# THE SECRET OF THE FORBIDDEN CONTINENT

"*Who was your father?*" the mutant asked Dale Kesley. And try as he might, Kesley could not remember; his past was an utter blank. But he knew one thing—the answer to his life's riddle lay in Antarctica, the once frozen continent, now an Earthly paradise surrounded by an impenetrable barrier.

But how to get there? The only available transportation were the spindly, six-legged mutant horses. And it would be suicide for Kesley to travel on the American continents. Two immortal dictators had set king-sized rewards for his capture — dead or alive.

But somewhere in the two continents there was someone who would help him, someone he had to find. The future of the world depended on his success!

*Features a new introduction by the author.*

# THE 13TH IMMORTAL

# ROBERT SILVERBERG

COSMOS BOOKS

# THE 13TH IMMORTAL

Published by
Dorchester Publishing Co., Inc.
200 Madison Ave.
New York, NY 10016
in collaboration with Wildside Press LLC

ISBN-10: 0-8439-5951-7
ISBN-13: 978-0-8439-5951-2

The name "Cosmos Books" and the Cosmos logo
are the property of Wildside Press, LLC.

Printed in the United States of America.

# INTRODUCTION

It was September of 1956, I was twenty-one years old, and all the doors of the world were opening for me at once.

That June I had graduated from college; my new career as a professional science-fiction writer was already well under way, with dozens of stories sold in the first year alone; in late August I married my college girlfriend and a week afterward, at the World Science Fiction Convention in New York, I was given a Hugo as the most promising new author of the year.

Then I went off with my bride to the first Milford Science Fiction Conference, where the writers I had begun to think of as my fellow professionals — Theodore Sturgeon, James Blish, Damon Knight, Fritz Leiber, Cyril Kornbluth, Frederik Pohl, Lester del Rey, Algis Budrys, and many others — treated me, the startlingly prolific newcomer, with respect and affection.

And now, with that dizzying rush of events behind me, I found myself established in a sprawling, handsome apartment on one of Manhattan's finest residential streets, embarking on real adult life — if you will accept the notion that there is anything real or adult about deciding, straight out of college, to earn one's livelihood by making up stories about the far reaches of space and time and getting publishers to pay for them.

I thought I could make it work.

I had already demonstrated, to myself and everyone else, that I could produce publishable material on a day-in-day-out basis, a steady stream of stories at a level of prolificity that only a few writers (Frederick Faust, George Simenon, Arthur J. Burks, L. Ron Hubbard, John Creasey) had ever matched. Story ideas were available to me at the snap of a finger and I had the youthful stamina needed to turn out twenty, thirty, even forty pages of fiction a day, five days a week, without faltering.

For the past eighteen months, even while I was finishing my senior year at Columbia, I had worked at that pace in the most matter-of-fact way, and I had sold everything I had written — not necessarily to the first magazine where I submitted it, but, sooner or later, someone had been willing to buy it.

Even in my youthful exuberance, though, I knew that it wouldn't be possible to sustain a full-time career indefinitely by writing short stories alone.

Allowing two or three days per story, sometimes even doing them at a single sitting, rarely if ever revising my first drafts, I could easily turn out somewhere between 100 and 150 stories a year — but where would I sell them all?

There were about a dozen science fiction magazines then, and I was selling regularly to all of them.

But the three highest paying magazines (*Astounding, Galaxy, Fantasy & SF*) were extremely demanding markets: I would be doing well to sell each of them as many as three stories a year against the competition of everyone else in the field. The lesser magazines, harder pressed to fill their pages, had shown a willingness to publish a story of mine in virtually every issue, sometimes two or even three.

But how long could I keep that up?

A couple of years, perhaps — but not forever.

The answer lay in writing novels. There were three main publishers of s-f novels in those days — Doubleday, Ballantine, and Ace.

Doubleday, the preserve of such top-level writers as Heinlein, Asimov, and Bradbury, was surely beyond my reach at that time.

Ballantine, the home of Sturgeon, Clarke, Pohl, John Wyndham, and Jack Vance, had no great need of my still immature talents either. But then there was Ace, a publishing house that was producing two double volumes a month, each offering a pair of 50,000-word novels bound back to back. I had heard that Ace was paying $1,000 per novel — substantial pay indeed, in an era when $100 a week was a decent wage and my splendid West End Avenue apartment cost me just $150 a month. And Ace, which put out more books a year than the other two houses combined, was always in need of new writers to meet its voracious publishing schedule.

A single 50,000-word book was the equivalent in length of eight or ten short stories, but how much easier it would be, I reasoned, to develop a single idea to book length than to produce eight or ten separate ideas as short stories and sell them all!

The book would bring in more money, too, since I could hope for no more than $50 or $75 a piece for most of those stories, assuming I sold them all right away.

And there would be the hope of translation income for a novel, besides — additional fees from France, Germany, or Italy, perhaps.

Having made all those calculations, I approached Donald A. Wollheim, the shrewd and experienced editor of Ace Books, right after my Hugo victory at the New York convention, and asked him whether he would be interested in adding me to his list of writers, which already included such established figures as Gordon R. Dickson, Poul Anderson, Philip K. Dick, and Leigh Brackett.

Wollheim sized me up quickly, seeing the mix of developing talent, unparalleled productiveness, and raw ambition that I was, and told me he'd be glad to take me on.

"Let me see a couple of chapters and an outline and I'll give you a contract," he said.

And so, on a warm September day right after my return from the Milford gathering, I got down to work.

My magnificent new apartment had scarcely any furniture in it, then, and I remember typing my opening chapters on a folding card table set up in the middle of an empty room.

My starting point was a mental image of the prototypical Ace novel as I understood it — a short, fast-moving book set a few hundred years in the future and rich in colorful description and melodramatic conflict.

What was required of me, I believed, was nothing at all like the coolly intellectual work of Isaac Asimov or the crisp, knowing manner of Robert A. Heinlein, or the insight into character of Theodore Sturgeon, or the poetic power of Ray Bradbury — just as well, because there was no way that I could begin to match those writers' skills at that time.

But I could and would do an Ace novel that would hold its own among other novels of its type, and, very quickly, a sketch for a book I called *The Years of the Freeze* took shape.

Wollheim liked my proposal and issued a contract immediately. It's dated October 10, 1956 — scarcely a month from the day I began writing the outline.

I wasted no time getting started on the book. I suspect I wrote it at a pace of 20 to 25 pages a day, which means the job would have taken me eight or nine working days, since the manuscript — I still have a carbon copy of it — runs to 206 pages. My journal shows that I finished it at in mid-November, 1956.

(Also that month I wrote the short stories "Quick Freeze," "Satellite Peril," "Sunrise on Mercury," "Spawn of the Void," "The Alien Menace," "Devil's World," the novella "Sea Lords of Forgotten Terra," and eight other items of various sorts.

Not just my head but my fingers start to ache at the thought of producing all that — using a manual typewriter, of course, since computers were still science fiction in 1956 and even electric typewriters were uncommon things.)

Wollheim liked the book, I guess — he immediately gave me a contract for a second novel, which would be called *Master of Life and Death* — and brought it out in the spring of 1957 as part of a double volume that also contained James Gunn's *This Fortress World*. Don was an inveterate title-changer — he was the editor who reprinted Stanley G. Weinbaum's story "Flight on Titan" as "A Man, a Maid, and Saturn's Temptation" — and my title *Years of the Freeze* gave way to Wollheim's *The Thirteenth Immortal*, which actually struck me as an improvement.

Here it is again, in print for the first time in forty-five years.

Maybe it isn't quite up there with such later books of mine as *Dying Inside* or *Lord Valentine's Castle*, but I beg you to remember that I was just twenty-one years old when I wrote it, and Shakespeare didn't turn out material like *Othello* or *King Lear* from the outset, either.

Looking through it now, I find it full of little touches of the kind that one day would be called Silverbergian, little bits of insight and color like the mutant colony in chapter nine — and it's an interesting literary curiosity besides.

Though the book may not exactly be of Hugo Award-winning caliber, I think it does foreshadow the novelist who was to come, and, at the very least, isn't it interesting to see how far a writer's career can go from a start like this?

—Robert Silverberg,
October, 2004

# THE 13TH
# IMMORTAL

# PROLOGUE

CENTURIES LATER, men would talk of those years as the Years of the Freeze. They would mean the years between 2062 ad 2527, the years when mankind, shattered by its own hand, maintained a rigid cultural stasis while rebuilding.

Those were the years when what was, would be. The years when there would be nothing new under the sun because mankind willed it so. The century of war, culminating in the almost total global destruction of 2062, had taught lessons that were not soon forgotten.

The old ways returned to the world — ways that had held sway for thousands of years, and which had regained ascendancy after the brief, nightmarish reign of the machine. Mankind still had machines, of course; life would have been impossible without them. But the Years of the Freeze were years of primarily hand labor, of travel by foot or by horse, of slow living and fear of complexity. The clock rolled back to an older, simpler kind of world — and froze there.

Like all ages, this one had its symbols and, conveniently, the symbols of the status quo were actual as well as symbolic forces in maintaining the Freeze. There were twelve of them — the Twelve Dukes, they called themselves, and they ruled the world between them. They had no power over the forgotten land of Antarctica, but otherwise they were virtually supreme. North America, South America, East and West Europe, Scandinavia, Australia, North Africa, Equatorial Africa, South Africa, China, India, Oceanica — each boasted its Duke.

They were products of the great blast of 2062, and they had found their way to power tortuously. Most of them had lived ordinary lives, picking their way through the wreckage with the others in the first three confused decades after the great destruction. But the others had died and the Twelve had not.

They had endured through forty, fifty, sixty years, themselves frozen indefinitely in middle life. And as the decades passed, each forced his way to control of a segment of the world. Each carved himself a Dukedom and, in 2162, the centennial of the Old World's death, they gathered together to divide the world among themselves.

There was a bitter struggle for power, but from it emerged the world of the Twelve Empires, stable, sedate, unchanging, determined never to allow the technology-born nightmare of old to return. The picture was attractive: twelve immortals, guiding the world along an even keel to the end of time.

Rumors filtered through the Twelve Empires occasionally that danger threatened from Antarctica. Man had redeemed Antarctica from the ice before the great cataclysm, and the polar land was known to be inhabited. But Antarctica remained detached from humanity, erecting an impassable barrier that cut itself off from the Twelve Empires as effectively as if it were on another planet. And so, the stasis held. The battered world rebuilt, on a more modest scale than of old, clinging to the simple ways, and froze that way. Here, there, an isolated city refused to participate in the Freeze. They, however, didn't matter. They intended to stay isolated, as did Antarctica, and the Twelve Dukes did not worry long over them.

In ninety percent of the world, time had stopped.

# ONE

HALF AN HOUR before the neat fabric of his life was to be shattered forever, Dale Kesley was thinking desperately, *This will be a good day for the planting*.

He stood at the end of a freshly-turned furrow, one brown hand gripping the sharebeam, the other patting the scaly gray flank of this mutant plough-horse. The animal neighed, a long croaking wheeze of a sound. Kesley looked down at the fertile soil of the furrow.

He was trying to tell himself that this was good land, that he had found a good place, here in the heart of Duke Winslow's sprawling farmland. He was compelling himself to believe that this was where he belonged, here where life held none of the uncertainty of the cities of the Twelve Empires. Right here where he had lived and worked for four years, here in Iowa Province.

But it was all wrong. Somewhere deep in the cloaked depths of his mind, he was trying to protest that there had been some mistake.

He wasn't a farmer.

He didn't belong in Iowa Province.

Somewhere, out there in the cities of the Twelve Empires, maybe in the radiation-blasted caves of the Old World, perhaps in the remote fastness of the unknown Antarctican empire, life was waiting for him.

Not here. Not in Iowa.

As always, a cold shudder ran through him and he let his head wobble as the sickness swept upward. He swayed, tightened his grip on the plough, and forced himself grimly back into the synthetic mood of security that was his one defense against the baseless terror that tormented him.

*The farm is good,* he thought.

*Everything here is good.*

Slowly, the congealed fear melted and drained away, and he felt whole again.

"Up, old hoss."

He slapped the flank and the horse neighed again and swished its bony tail. It was a good horse too, he thought fiercely. Somehow, everything was good now, even the old horse.

Experienced hands had warned him against buying a mutie, but when he'd bought the half-share of the farm he had had to do it. The Old Kind were few and well spaced in Iowa Province, and all too expensive. They fetched upward of five thousand dollars at the markets; a good solid mutie went for only five hundred.

Besides, Kesley had argued, the Old Kind belonged with the Old World — dead five hundred years, and long covered with dust. Only the distant towers of New York still blazed with radiation; the chain reaction there would continue through all eternity, as a warning and a threat. But Kesley wasn't concerned with that.

He started down a new furrow, guiding the plough smoothly and well, strong arms gripping the beam while the horse moved steadily onward. In front of him, the broad expanse of Iowa Province stretched out till it looked like it reached to the end of the world. The brown land rolled on endlessly, stopping only where it ran into the hard blueness of the cloudless sky.

Suddenly, the horse whinnied sharply. Kesley stiffened. The old mutie could smell trouble half a mile away. Kesley had learned to value the animal's warning. He stepped out from behind the plough and looked around. The horse whinnied again and raked the unbroken ground with its forepaws.

Kesley shaded his eyes and squinted. Far down at the other end of the field, near the rock fence that separated his land from Loren's, a dark-blue animal was slinking unobtrusively over the ground.

*Blue wolf.*

*And today I'll have your hide, old henstealer,* Kesley thought jubilantly.

He patted the horse's flank once again and started to run, crouching low, moving silently across the bare field. The wolf hadn't seen him yet. The blue-furred creature was edging across the field down below, probably heading past the farmhouse to rob the poultry yard.

A daylight raid? Times must be bad, Kesley thought. The blue wolf normally struck only at night. Well, something had brought the old wolf out in broad daylight, and this time Kesley would nail him.

He circled sharply, staying downwind of the animal and stepped up his pace. Without breaking stride, he unsheathed his knife and gripped it tightly. The wolf was nearly the size of a man; if Kesley caught up with him, it would be a bloody fight for both of them. But a wolf's hide was a treasure well worth a few scratches.

The wolf caught the scent, now, and began to run up the path toward the farmhouse. Kesley realized the animal was confused, was running into a dead end.

So much the better. He'd kill the beast in the sight of Loren and the farm wenches and old Lester.

He clenched his teeth and kept running. The wolf looked back at him, bared its mouthful of yellow daggers, snarled. Its blue fur seemed to glitter in the bright morning sunlight.

Kesley's breath was starting to come hard as he ascended the steep hill that led to the farmhouse. He slackened just a bit; he'd need to conserve his strength for the battle to come.

As he reached the crest of the hill, he saw Loren stick his head out of the second floor of the farmhouse.

"Hey, Dale!"

Kesley pointed up ahead. "Wolf!" he grunted.

The animal was drawing close to the poultry yard now. Kesley stepped up his clip again. He wanted to catch it just as it passed the door of the farmhouse. He wanted to nail it there, to plunge the knife into its heart and —

Abruptly, a strange figure stepped out of the farmhouse door. In one smooth motion, the figure put hand to hip, drew forth a blaster, fired. The wolf paused in midstride as if frozen, shuddered once, and dropped. There was the sickening smell of burning fur in the air.

Kesley felt a quick burst of hot anger. He looked down at the smouldering ruin of the wolf huddled darkly against the ground, then to the stranger, who was smiling as he reholstered the blaster.

"What the hell did you do that for?" Kesley demanded hotly. "Who asked you to shoot? What are you doing here, anyway?"

He raised his knife in a wild threatening gesture. The stranger moved tentatively toward his hip again, and Kesley quickly relaxed. He lowered his knife, but continued to glare bitterly at the stranger.

"A thousand pardons, young friend." The newcomer's voice was deep and resonant, and somehow oily-sounding. "I had no idea the wolf was yours. I merely acted out of reflex. I understand it's customary for farmers to kill wolves on sight. Believe me, I thought I was helping you."

The stranger was dressed in courtly robes that contrasted sharply with Kesley's simple farmer's muslin. He wore a flowing cape of red trimmed with yellow gilt, a short stiff beard stained red to match, and a royal blue tunic. He was tall and powerful looking, with wide-set black eyes and heavy, brooding eyebrows that ran in a solid bar across his forehead.

"I don't care if you *are* from the court," Kesley snapped. "That wolf was mine. I chased it up from the fields — and to have some city bastard step out of nowhere and ruin my kill for me just as I'm —"

*Dale!"*

The sharp voice belonged to Loren Harker, Kesley's farming partner, a veteran fieldsman, tall and angular, face dried by the sun and skin brown and tough. He appeared from the farmhouse door and stood next to the stranger.

Kesley realized he had spoken foolishly. "I'm — sorry," he said, his voice unrepentant. "It's just that it boiled me to see — dammit, you had no *business* doing that!"

"I understand," the stranger said calmly. "It was a mistake on my part. Please accept my apologies."

"Accepted," Kesley muttered. Then his eyes narrowed suspiciously. "Say, what kind of tax-collector are you, anyway? You're the first man out of Duke Winslow's court who ever said anything but *'Give me'*."

"Tax-collector? Why call me that?"

"Why else would you come to the farmlands, if not for the tithe? Don't play games," Kesley said impatiently. He kicked the worthless wolf-carcass to one side and stepped between Loren and the stranger. "Come on inside, and tell me how much I owe my liege lord this time."

"You don't understand —" Loren started to say, but the stranger put one hand on his shoulder and halted him.

"Let me," he said.

He turned to Kesley. "I'm not a tax-collector. I'm not from the court of Duke Winslow at all."

"What are you doing in farm country, then?"

The stranger smiled evenly. "I came here because I'm looking for someone. But what are *you* doing here, Dale Kesley?"

The question was like a stinging slap in the face. For a moment, Kesley remained frozen, unreacting. Then, as the words penetrated below the surface, a shadow of pain crossed his face. His mouth sagged open.

*What are you doing here, Dale Kesley?*

The words blurred and re-echoed like a shout in a cavern. Kesley felt suddenly naked, as the mask of self-deception and hypocrisy that had erected itself during his four years in Iowa Province crumbled inward and fell away. It was the one question he had dreaded to face.

"You look sick," Loren said. "What's wrong, Dale?" The older man's voice was hushed, bewildered.

"Nothing," Kesley said hesitantly. "Nothing at all." But he was unable to meet the stranger's calm smile and, worse, he had no idea why.

His thoughts flashed back to that moment at the plough earlier that morning, when Iowa had seemed like the universe and he had made life appear infinitely good.

*Lies.*

Farm life was his natural state, he had pretended. He *belonged* behind the plough, here in Iowa.

*Lies.*

But — where *did* he belong?

He realized that he was acting irrationally. Loren's face hung before him, uncomprehending, frightened. The stranger seemed almost gloatingly self-confident.

"What did you mean by that?" Kesley asked, slowly. His voice sounded harsh and unfamiliar in his own ears.

"Have you ever been in the cities?" the stranger asked, ignoring Kesley's question.

"Once, maybe twice. I don't like it there. I'm a farmer; always have been. I came down from Kansas Province. But what the hell —?"

The stranger raised one hand to silence him. An amused twinkle crossed the cold black eyes, and the thin lips curved upward. "They did a good job," the stranger said, half to himself. "You really believe you're a farmer, don't you, Dale? Have been, all your life?"

Again the words stung; they bit deep into a hidden reservoir of fear, and rose to the surface again, leaving Kesley strangely disturbed. "Yes," he said stubbornly. "What are you trying to do?" Anger came over him again, and he snapped, "Suppose I order you off my farm?"

The stranger laughed. "*Your* farm?" His eyes probed searchingly. "How can you call this *your* farm?"

Kesley quailed at the incomprehensible pain this third attack brought. *What is he after? Why can't he leave me alone?*

*This is my farm.*

*I belong here.*

He stood poised, swaying on the balls of his feet, staring mystifiedly at his tormentor. *I belong here*, he thought fiercely — but without any conviction, this time. Something within his mind kept insisting that it was a lie, that he belonged elsewhere.

The glitter of the cities suddenly rose as an image in his mind.

Rage boiled over. "Let me alone!" he shouted, and jumped forward, raising the knife high.

*"No!"*

The stranger's voice was almost a shriek of fear, but he was cool enough to draw and fire. A bright spurt of flame nudged from the muzzles of the blaster, and Kesley felt a sudden intolerable warmth in his hand. He dropped the hot knife and stepped back, panting like a trapped tiger.

"I wish you hadn't done that," the stranger said.

"I wish you had never come here," Kesley retorted. It was like a nightmare. He felt blind, unable to defend himself, unable even to understand the source of the attack.

Loren was watching the scene in utter horror, and Kesley noticed a couple of the farm girls standing a short distance away, watching, too. The stranger stood with arms folded.

"Let's go inside," he suggested. "We can talk better in there."

Kesley remained rooted, unable to think, unable to

move. "This is my farm," he said out loud, after a moment. "Isn't it?" It was nearly a whimper.

The harshness vanished abruptly from the stranger's face. Kesley watched uncomprehendingly as hard lines, melted, sharp cheekbones no longer seemed so austere. It was the eyes, he thought curiously. They controlled the expression of the face. And now the cold eyes seemed to radiate warmth.

"Of course this is your farm," the stranger said. He gripped Kesley's arm. "They really did a job on you, didn't they?"

"They?"

"Never mind. I don't want to hurt you any more than I have already. Let's go inside, and we can talk about it there."

Word had somehow travelled rapidly around the farm, and within minutes the farmhouse living room was crowded with curious people. Kesley looked around. He saw Loren, and toothless old Lester, who had owned the farm once and sold it to Loren and Kesley. There were Lester's three daughters, brawny, tanned girls who did the women's work on the farm. There was Tim, the slow-witted hired hand.

And there was the stranger in the gilt-bordered red cloak. The stranger glanced from one face to another, then at Kesley. "Can we talk in privacy?"

"You heard what he said," Kesley snapped to the others. "Get about your jobs."

"You sure you want us to leave you alone?" Loren asked. "You looked pretty wobbly a minute ago out there, and —"

"Don't cross me, Loren!"

The older man shrugged. "You're the boss, Dale. Come on, Tim, let's leave them alone."

"Pretty nice city clothes he's got," old Lester cackled.

Tina, Lester's oldest daughter, nudged him scornfully. "Let's get moving, Lester. The *men* want to talk." She indicated with a smirk her disapproval of the exclusion order.

When the others were gone, Kesley turned to the stranger.

"We're alone. Now tell me who you are and what you want with me."

The stranger tugged at his stiff red beard for a moment.

"I'm Dryle van Alen. Does that enlighten you?"

"Not at all. Where are you from?"

"The Dukedom of Antarctica," van Alen said.

For the second time in half an hour, Kesley did a double take. The words sank in slowly, burrowed into his mind — and then exploded into pinwheeling brilliance.

*"Antarctica!"*

"Why the surprise?" van Alen asked mildly. "There are people in Antarctica too, you know. You'd think I had said Mars, or some other impossible place."

"If this is a joke, van Alen, I'm going to feed you to the hogs with tomorrow's swill."

"It's no joke. I'm attached to the court of the Duke of Antarctica."

"So they've got a Duke, too," Kesley said. He smiled. "I never thought that they'd have one just like us. And I suspect the Twelve Dukes don't even know that. But this is crazy! If you're from Antarctica, what do you want with me?"

"All in good time," van Alen said calmly. "First: the Twelve Dukes are very much aware of the existence of their Antarctic confrere. He is, like them, an immortal. Unlike them, he is not interested in striving for power."

"Why does Antarctica cut itself off from the rest of the world?"

"A matter of choice," van Alen said. "Our Duke doesn't care for the company of his twelve colleagues, nor for that of their subjects. But you're leading me astray with your questions. You're not letting me explain why I came here to you."

"Go ahead, then." Kesley sat back, trying to conceal his tenseness.

It made no sense at all. The Twelve Dukes had ruled the world four hundred years, and in that time no contact between men of the Twelve Empires and the people of the continent of Antarctica had ever taken place. A barrier had always surrounded that continent. Antarctica was as unapproachable as frozen Pluto, or one of the stars.

And now the barrier had lowered long enough to let this Dryle van Alen out into the world of the Twelve

Dukes. Van Alen had made his way to America, to Duke Winslow's land — merely to see Dale Kesley? It was impossible.

Van Alen peered at Kesley. "You have lived in Iowa Province for four years — is that right?"

Kesley nodded.

"And before that, where?"

"Kansas Province. I was a farmer there, too."

One of van Alen's heavy eyebrows twitched skeptically.

"Oh? How long did you live in Kansas Province, then?"

"All my life. I was born there. I lived there twenty-one years. I came here four years ago. "

Van Alen chuckled. "You cling to that story the way you would a straw in a maelstrom." He leaned forward; his voice deepened. "Suppose you try to tell me why you left Kansas Province to come here."

"Why, I —"

Kesley paused. A muscle began to throb painfully in one cheek, and he looked down at his heavy work-boots in confusion. He had no answer. He did not know.

Once again, the same malaise that had spread over him outside hit him. He sucked in a deep breath, but said nothing.

"You don't know why you left Kansas?" van Alen asked gently. "Think, Dale. Try to remember."

Kesley clenched his fists, fighting to keep back a cry of rage and frustration and fear. Finally he said, "I don't

know. I don't remember. That's it — I don't remember."
His voice was glacially calm.

"Very good. You don't remember." Van Alen tugged
at his beard again, as if to signify that he had won
a telling point. "Next question: describe in detail your
life in Kansas Province. What your farm was like, what
your mother looked like, how tall your father was —
little things like that. Eh?" The questions poured down
on Kesley like an unstoppable torrent; they seemed
to wash his feet out from under him and leave him
struggling helplessly and impotently to regain his foot-
ing.

"My mother? My father? I —"

Again he stopped. The room was blurred; only the
smiling, diabolical face of the Antarctican seemed to be
fixed, and all else was whirling. Kesley elbowed himself
up from his chair and crossed the room in two quick
bounds.

"Damn you, I don't remember! *I don't remember!*"

He grabbed van Alen roughly by the scruff of his
cloak and hauled him to his feet.

"Let go of me, Dale."

The sharp command was all but impossible not to
obey, but Kesley, shaking hysterically, continued to
hold tight. He clutched for the Antarctican's throat,
burning to choke the life out of this torturer before he
could ask any more questions.

His hands touched the skin of the Antarctican's
throat and then, quite coolly, van Alen broke Kesley's

grip. He did it easily, simply grasping the wrists with his own long fingers and lifting.

Kesley struggled, but to no avail. The Antarctican was fantastically strong. Kesley writhed in his grip, but could not break loose. Slowly, without apparent effort, van Alen forced him to his knees and let go.

Kesley made no attempt to rise. He was beaten — physically and mentally. Van Alen stooped, lifted him, eased him to the couch. Drawing forth a scented handkerchief, he mopped perspiration first from Kesley's forehead, then from his own.

"That was unpleasant," van Alen remarked.

Kesley remained slumped on the couch.

"You shouldn't have tried to attack me, Dale. I'm here to help you."

"How?" Kesley asked tonelessly.

"I'm here to show you the way hack to your home."

"My home's in Kansas Province." Stubbornly.

"Your home is in Antarctica, Dale. You might as well admit to yourself now."

Strangely, the words had little effect on Kesley. He had already been shocked past any point of surprise.

For four years, he had been persuading himself that he had come from Kansas Province. He had gone on thinking that, all the while subliminally aware that there was no rational reason for that belief, that he had no memories of his earlier life whatever.

Kansas Province had seemed as likely a homeland as any, and he had clung to the idea. As each year passed, it had seemed more and more the truth to him — until van Alen came.

Now he was ready to believe anything. The barriers were down.

"Antarctica?" he repeated.

Van Alen nodded. "You've been the subject of the most intensive manhunt in the history of humanity." That seemed to amuse him; he stopped, chuckled. "A history, to be sure, that stretches back all of four hundred years — but a history, nevertheless. Dale, we've searched through every one of the Twelve Empires for you. You were finally located here, in Iowa Province. The search is over; it took four years."

"I'm happy for you," Kesley said. "You must be pleased to have found me." His voice was restrained, matter-of-fact. "So the search is over?"

"Partially," van Alen said. "We have the treasure, now; we lack only the key to the box. Daveen the Singer, the blind man. The search for him continues."

Kesley frowned impatiently. "What the hell is this all about, van Alen?"

Van Alen smiled warmly. "I'm sorry, Dale. I can't tell you anything, not until Daveen has been found. But that can't take long, now that we've located you."

"Who's this Daveen?"

"A poet," van Alen said. "Also a remarkably skilled hypnotist. We'll find him soon, and then the search will really be over." The Antarctican seemed to be gazing *through* Kesley, as if he were staring all the way to his distant homeland. His eyes had turned cold again; his face had hardened.

"Suppose I tell you you're a lunatic?" Kesley asked.

"Suppose you do," van Alen said animatedly. "You'd have every right to the opinion. Care to join me in lunacy?"

"Eh?"

"Will you come with me — to Antarctica?"

"I'm not *that* crazy," Kesley said. He laughed. "You want me to drop everything — the farm, my whole life, just to go off with you to — to *Antarctica?*"

"This is not your life," van Alen said. "Antarctica is. Will you come?"

Kesley laughed contemptuously, but said nothing.

There was a knock on the door.

"Come on," he said roughly. "Enter."

Tina came in and looked defiantly at both of them. She was a tall, red-haired girl in her late twenties, wide-shouldered and high-bosomed, and her eyes held the flash and fire that must have belonged to old Lester once. She and Kesley had been sharing a room for six months.

"Still talking?" Tina asked.

"Is there anything special you want?" Kesley snapped.

"Just wanted to tell you lunch is getting cold, that's all. And you left your plough standing in the field. That crazy mutie horse of yours looks like it's asleep on its feet."

Kesley frowned. "Tell Tim to go down there and finish the furrow, will you? I'll be in for lunch in a couple of minutes."

Tina glanced curiously toward van Alen and said, "With or without company?"

"I'll be leaving in a few minutes," van Alen told her. "You needn't prepare anything for me."

"Sorry to hear that," Tina said acidly. "We were looking forward to feeding you." She turned and flounced out.

"Who's that?" van Alen asked.

"Lester's daughter — Lester's the old man. Her name's Tina. She lives with me."

There was a visible stiffening of van Alen's manner. Leaning forward anxiously, he said, "You — have no children yet, have you?"

"You kidding? That's all I need. Things are complicated enough around here without —"

Van Alen rose abruptly. "I see. Well, I'll have to be leaving now, Dale." He wrapped his cloak around his shoulders tightly and walked across the living room. "It's going to be a long hard journey to the Pole; I must begin at once."

He put his hand to the door. Kesley watched him open it.

"Hold it, van Alen. Don't go."

"Why?"

Kesley shook his head without replying. Van Alen looked at him for a moment, shrugged, and turned a second time to leave.

Without really knowing why he was doing what he was about to do, Kesley cupped his hands. *"Tina!"*

The girl reappeared and confronted him quizzically.

"Get upstairs and pack my things," Kesley ordered her. "I'm leaving."

"Leaving?"

"Right this minute," he said. "I'm leaving with *him*." He pointed squarely at van Alen.

# Two

CITY NOISES — the dizzying chaos of the metropolis. Kesley and van Alen reined in their mounts at the gates of the city of Galveston, capital of Texas Province and a main bastion of Duke Winslow of North America.

It seemed to Kesley that they had been riding for months. Actually, it had been only a matter of weeks for the long ride through the farmlands, down through Texas to the Gulf.

They moved along now at a slow canter, guiding their horses into a line that disappeared between the heavy copper gates surrounding the walled city. Galveston was an encircled peninsula, guarded by land, open to the sea.

Men in the green and gold uniforms of Duke Winslow's guard rode alongside the line, keeping the jostling crowd in order.

"Better get your coins ready," van Alen muttered, as they drew near the gate.

"Coins?"

"This is a fee city. A dollar a head to enter the gate." Kesley made a face and dug a golden dollar from his pocket. He looked at the tiny, well-worn coin almost wistfully. "The good Duke takes care that his subjects are never weighted with overmuch coinage," he observed. "The Duke's men relieve us of it joyfully."

They rode past the gate. A sleepy-eyed toll-keeper sat, impassively watching, as each newcomer to the city deposited his dollar in the till.

As Kesley passed the tollbox, he flipped the coin in casually. It clinked against several of the others, spun, and bounced out, rolling some ten feet away. Kesley shrugged apologetically and continued ahead.

"Hey there!" The guard's voice was loud and harsh. "Get down there and —"

The voice of the toll-keeper died away. Kesley looked around and saw van Alen down on his knees in the well-trampled mud, rooting in the filth for the coin. The noble man seemed to show no compunction about crawling before the toll-keeper.

"Here you are, sir." Van Alen obsequiously deposited Kesley's dollar in the tollbox, added one of his own, and handed a third coin to the toll-keeper.

"The boy is sick," van Alen murmured, gesturing significantly. "He does not know what he does."

The toll-keeper nodded curtly and pocketed the dollar. "Get moving, both of you," he snapped.

Kesley, who had trotted a few feet further, halted to let van Alen catch up with him.

"That's a good way to assure a short life," the Antarctican said. "Toll-keepers are notorious for their quick triggers. Don't make needless trouble for yourself, boy."

"Sorry," Kesley said. "It riled me to see him sitting

there so smug and taking our money. I didn't really mean to throw the coin on the ground."

Van Alen shook his head sadly. "It riled you," he repeated, his voice mocking. "You've been lucky so far — each time you've lost your temper, you've survived. But better learn to curb it. These people are your superiors, whether you like it or not, and if a Duke wants a dollar to enter his city, you put down your dollar or you ride the other way."

"Superiors, hell! They've got no right —"

"You're just so much dirt, Kesley," the Antarctican said with sudden force. Oddly, the words did not stir Kesley to anger. "Learn that lesson now. Whatever you may think you are, that doesn't alter the fact that you're nothing more than dirt."

Kesley swallowed hard, but said nothing. Van Alen was right, he was forced to admit. The Twelve Dukes ruled supreme, and beneath them came a complex and sharply-defined hierarchy in which, as a farmer, Kesley was close to the bottom. He had no call to flare up at toll-keepers.

But yet —

He shook his head. The fact of his insignificance was one he could accept intellectually, but he couldn't *believe* in it. And he never would. He had never been able to master the trick of lying to himself.

"What's on the schedule in Galveston?" Kesley asked, as they rode into the town. They entered a wide, crowded thoroughfare; mechanical transportation was forbidden in most parts of North America, but there were plenty of horsecarts and carriages — most of them drawn by variegated mutants of one sort or another, but a few by authentic horses of the Old Kind.

"We'll stay here overnight," van Alen said. "Tomorrow we pick up the steamer for South America. From there, it's straight down to Antarctica."

"And then?" Kesley prodded.

"And then you'll be in Antarctica."

That was all the information van Alen would ever give. From time to time on the trip down from Iowa, Kesley had found himself wondering just why he had pulled up roots and struck off with van Alen.

It was probably a combination of factors. Curiosity, certainly. Antarctica was the world's great mystery, keeping itself utterly aloof from the doings of the Twelve Empires. And then there was the vague unease he had felt during his stay in Iowa, the knowledge that he belonged somewhere else. And there was a third factor, too — a kind of randomness, a compulsive but seemingly unmotivated action whose nature he did not understand. He had agreed to come — that was all. *Why* never entered into it for long.

He was being led. Well, he would follow, and wait for the threads to untangle themselves.

Right now he was in a city for, supposedly, the third time in his life. He had the biographical data down pat: three years ago he had gone to market in Des Moines for his horse, and a year later he had made the trek down to St. Louis to sell grain. Both times he had been repelled by the bigness and squalor of the city. He felt the same emotion now.

But, as had happened the two previous times, there was also the feeling that the city, not the farm, was his natural habitat.

The street before them seemed familiar, though he knew he had never been in Galveston before. It stretched far out of sight, bordered on both sides by low, square, old houses and brightly-colored shops. Hawkers yelled stridently in the roadway, peddling fruits and vegetables and here and there some comely wench's favors.

Van Alen pointed toward a rickety building on their right and said, "There's a hotel. Let's room up for the night."

"Good enough," Kesley agreed.

The proprietor of the hotel was a short man, in his early fifties, chubby and prosperous-looking, with an oily stubble of beard darkening his face. His bald head gleamed; it had been newly waxed.

"Hail, friends. In search of lodgings?"

"Indeed we are," van Alen said. "My friend and I are tired, and can use some rest."

The hotelman chuckled. "One room?"

"Suitable," van Alen said.

A thick eyebrow lifted. "Will you boys be needing a double bed?"

"What the hell do you mean —" Kesley began hotly, but van Alen cut him off and said in a calm voice, "Twin beds will be fine, if you've got them."

"Of course," the proprietor said. "Beg pardon." He reached behind him and fumbled on a board laden with keys, mumbling cheerfully to himself. Finally he decided on an appropriate room and unhooked the keys.

"Three-fifty," he said.

Van Alen placed four one-dollar pieces face upward on the desk. The hotelman looked at the coins, grinned, and scooped them up, putting a fifty-cent piece in their place. Van Alen ignored it, and after a moment the hotelman scooped that up as well.

"Come this way, please."

He showed them to a room on the third floor, which was the topmost. It was a boxy, green-walled room with a single naked fluorescent running along its ceiling. Kesley had vaguely hoped that the room would have floor-to-ceiling luminescence, as some of the oldest city hotels were reputed to have, but no such luck. This one had been built since the Blast; no fancy trimmings here.

There were two beds, both without spreads. The part of the sheet that was visible at the top was gray and frayed, though apparently clean. A slatted screen stood folded between the beds.

"Cozy, isn't it?" the proprietor asked. He seemed to be oozing filth. "It's one of our best doubles."

"Glad to hear it," van Alen said. "We've traveled far. We're tired."

"You'll rest well here," the hotelman said, and backed out the door.

"A greasy customer," Kesley commented when he was gone.

"No more so than usual," said van Alen. "They seem to be a breed. He means well, though." The Antarctican shrugged out of his cloak and draped it over a chair. Casually he unfolded the screen, dividing the room in half.

"Economy calls for a single room," he explained. "But privacy is still a fine thing."

Kesley shrugged. He had no intention of violating any of van Alen's personal crotchets. Approaching his own bed, he turned down the sheet, slipped off his clothing, and climbed in.

He discovered he had no desire to sleep. After tossing restlessly for a while, he rolled over on his back and sat up. "Van Alen?"

"What is it, Kesley?"

"How big is Galveston?"

"About a hundred thousand people," van Alen said. "It's a very big city."

"Oh." After a pause: "Bet New York was much bigger, wasn't it?"

"Cities were bigger in the old days. Too big. It drove people mad to live in them. That's why the cities were destroyed. Your Dukes make sure the same thing doesn't happen again by building walls around the cities. Galveston won't ever get any bigger than it is."

"Is that the way things are in Antarctica, too?"

"You'll find out about Antarctica when you get there. Go to sleep — or at least let me sleep."

Van Alen sounded irritated. The Antarctican was a queer duck, Kesley thought, as he lay awake in the silence. Van Alen was a slick operator, calm and self-assured, but there were strange chinks in his armor. He blew up, occasionally, lost his temper — not often, but sometimes. And there were many questions he would not answer, and others that seemed to disturb him more than they should.

He conducted himself strangely, too — doing things almost without motivation, it seemed, though Kesley felt that deep calculations lay behind the seemingly gratuitous acts. Such things as picking the first hotel they saw, or tipping the proprietor a needless half dollar. They stood out sharply against the fabric of reality. They were unnecessary actions — or were they?

Kesley didn't know. And Kesley resolved, in that moment, not to try to find out. He would abrogate all responsibility, let happen what might. It was the only way to ward off the terrors of unanswerable questions. Away from his home, away from the farm, he simply was not equipped to act independently — *yet*. He decided to sit tight, ask no questions, and look for no answers.

They left Galveston early the next morning, via the *Snowden*, a creaky old second-class freight-steamer, carrying eight other passengers and a small herd of cattle on their way to Cuba. Van Alen had made all the traveling arrangements; Kesley, having no idea how such things were managed, had done nothing.

The ship docked at Havana, discharged its load of kine, and moved unsteadily southward. From Havana to Merida, in Yucatan; from Merida to Panama. The charred wreckage of the old canal was gauntly visible as they steamed past the Isthmus.

Skirting the east coast of South America, the *Snowden* pulled into port at Bahia Blanca, in Argentina Province — and here, van Alen and Kesley disembarked.

"This is as far south as any ship goes," van Alen said, as the tug drew them toward the dreary harbor. "The rest of the trip is overland."

"To Antarctica? How?"

Van Alen smiled. "Overland through Argentina, at any rate, and down into Patagonia. There'll be transportation waiting for us there."

Fifteen minutes later, they were waiting at the customs shed for their horses. A bored-looking little customs official in blue shorts and gold brocaded jacket approached them, clutching a clipboard and a stubby pencil.

"Where are you from?" His voice was thickly accented but understandable.

"North America," van Alen said. "We're vassals of His Liege Duke Winslow."

The customs man scribbled something on his clipboard. "You are now in the lands of His Highness Don Miguel, Sovereign Ruler and Duke of South and Central America. Entrance fee to His Highness' lands is for you ten dollar American. You have?"

Kesley scowled but produced the fee without question. Van Alen handed money over as well. The customs officer smiled coldly and nodded.

"Very well. You may enter. There will be no inspection of your belongings."

"Trusting fellow, isn't he?" Kesley asked, as they saddled their animals. "No customs inspection."

"They're very trusting down here, especially, when you give them ten dollars too many. Don Miguel's Dukedom isn't particularly noted for its high ethical standards, Kesley. Everyone's fantastically loyal to the Duke, but they stay loyal to themselves as well. See?"

"You know, you've spent more cash in bribes on this trip than I've ever seen in my life," Kesley said.

"A well-greased road makes for a smooth journey," van Alen intoned. "Another important lesson for you."

Kesley smiled and goaded his horse on. The road out of Bahia Blanca was a long and winding one; from this vantagepoint, Argentina Province looked limitless. The air was cold and clear, down in this continent where winter came in July. Kesley let the constant rhythm of his galloping horse lull him into a veiled patience; he rode impassively, listening to the repeated *clickety-clack* of well-shod hooves coming from van Alen's Old Kind horse, and the less distinct, thumping sound of his own mutant steed's three-toed paws pounding the roadway. The sounds tended to hypnotize him. At any rate, they kept him from thinking too seriously about the unknown destination that lay ahead.

The journey continued. By evening of the next day they had left the city far behind and had ridden into the heart of a broad, apparently endless, green plain covered thickly with coarse, matted grass and dotted with short, heavy-holed trees. Conversation between the two men had long since dwindled to a mere interchange of grunts.

But the monotony of the journey was short-lived. Near midnight, from over a slight rise in the plain, eight men appeared, riding lowslung mutant ponies. They were heading straight for van Alen and Kesley.

Kesley saw them first. He nudged van Alen.

"Bandits," the Antarctican said immediately. "Let's split up. You go to the east; I'll head the other way."

"And how do we get together again?"

"I'll find you afterward. Get going!"

Kesley dug in his spurs and the horse leaped forward. The bandits bore down on them as the two men rode in opposite directions. And, to Kesley's horror, he saw the bandit group splitting in two.

Instantly, van Alen doubled back and beckoned to Kesley to do the same. If the bandits had detected the maneuver and were sweeping off to intercept them, there was nothing gained by dividing. They stood a better chance back-to-back.

Together, then, they struck out along a side-path toward a thick copse. Kesley's hand slipped down from the bridle to feel the comforting hilt of his knife at his waist. He glanced at van Alen, and saw that the Antarctican's blaster gleamed dully, ready for use, in the man's hand.

The eight bandits drew up in a tight phalanx facing the copse. They were swarthy, dark-skinned men with heavy mustaches.

"Off your horse," van Alen whispered.

Kesley slipped to the ground and began to tether the mutant to a low-hanging branch.

"No," the Antarctican said harshly. "Let the animals roam free. Their noise will confuse the bandits."

"Right."

He released his grip on the reins and slapped the beast affectionately. The swaybacked mutant began to amble off into the depths of the copse, crashing down on fallen branches as it went. Van Alen's horse struck out in another direction. Kesley grinned suddenly; the sight of his clumsy old horse thrashing away into the darkness was utterly ludicrous.

Then Kesley glanced back at van Alen. The Antarctican was kneeling in a soft mossbank, aiming his blaster.

He squeezed the firing stud. A bright beam of light licked out. The horse of the leading bandit whinnied and looked down in amazement at the pastern that was no longer there, and then toppled, dropping its rider.

Van Alen fired again and a second horse went down. At that the bandits scattered. The two men on foot hit the ground; the other six rode off around the copse.

A loud report sounded from the left, followed by an

agonized neigh of pain. Kesley stiffened. *They shot my horse*, he thought. For some reason, hot tears of rage came to his eyes. The awkward-looking mutant horse had been a good friend for four years. Kesley felt as if his last bond with Iowa Province had just been severed.

He yanked out his knife. Pale moonlight flickered on the polished blade. Van Alen tapped Kesley's arm, shook his head cautioningly. Kesley saw the Antarctican aim the blaster.

Another spurt of light. The smell of singed leaves, sharp and acrid — and then, the smell of singed human flesh. A dull groan.

"That's one," van Alen muttered. "Seven to go."

Branches rustled behind them. Kesley whirled and raised his knife, but it was only van Alen's horse returning to its master. At a gesture from van Alen, Kesley slapped the steed's rump and sent it roaming again. Overhead, hoarse-voiced birds chattered their angry commentary on the conflict below.

The blaster spurted again, and in its sudden light Kesley saw a shadowed figure outside the copse char and fall.

Kesley began to perspire. There were still six bandits at large out there, and eventually van Alen's blaster would run out of charges.

Another bullet came whistling through the woods and thunked into a tree overhead.

"They've spotted the source of the beam," van Alen said. "Let's get moving."

"Where to?"

"Anywhere. We've got to misdirect them. I've only got two charges left."

Again came the rustling of branches behind them. *Van Alen's horse again,* Kesley thought, but this time he was wrong. The bandits were upon them.

All six at once — making a suicide charge on the man with the blaster. They came piling into the copse on foot, swarming around Kesley and van Alen, leaping and clawing and punching.

Van Alen's blaster spurted once, and a sharp-featured bandit took the charge in his stomach. He pitched forward on the Antarctican, who tried desperately to wriggle out from under the corpse. He did — but not before another bandit had seized the hand that held the blaster. There was a bright flare overhead suddenly, and the birds shrieked wildly. With an angry curse at having wasted the last charge, van Alen broke free of the man and hurled the useless blaster away. Meanwhile Kesley found himself busy. His knife dripped red; he had slashed it into one man's arm, then ripped downward. Another had seized his wrist as he drew back for a second thrust.

Kesley grimaced and groped for the other man's eyes. In the darkness of the copse not even the moon aided vision; it was impossible to see more than a foot or so, and Kesley contended with half-seen shapes rather than men.

The bandit twisted upward sharply. A bolt of pain

shot through Kesley's arm. Numbed, he let the knife slip from his grasp. It vanished underfoot.

"Dale?" The half-grunt came from van Alen, somewhere to the left. "The blaster's dead."

"And I've lost my knife!"

"Try to get free. If we can slip through them and outside the copse, we can grab their horses and —"

"We also speak English, *norteamericano*," a wry voice said suddenly. "Your strategy is no secret."

Kesley turned and jammed a fist into someone's stomach. He felt arms groping for his arms, and shrugged himself free. He stepped back, kicking out with his heavy boot.

His foot struck — but as it did, someone else hit him from behind and knocked him off balance. He slipped, rolled over and tried to pull himself up. Three men were on him in an instant, pinioning him.

He heard the click of a gun's safety going off, and a quiet voice said, "Hold fast or we will explode your head."

Instantly Kesley stiffened. "I'm holding fast," he said. He saw no point in resisting, not with three men squatting on him and a gun pointed at his head.

A short distance away the sound of struggle could still be heard. *Good for van Alen*, Kesley thought.

A knife flashed suddenly. A man howled: "Ricardo, you have cut *me!*" Angrily, in Spanish.

*Spanish? Where did I learn Spanish?* Kesley wondered.

He heard van Alen's ironic chuckle. "How are you doing, Kesley?"

"I'm caught. They're sitting on me."

A pause. Then; "Too bad, Dale." van Alen's deep voice sounded distant and troubled now. "I'm going to have to —"

His voice broke off abruptly. After a moment of silence, Kesley heard footsteps pounding rapidly away through the forest. Van Alen running away? *Why?*

One of the bandits fired. The forest was illuminated briefly by the flash of gunpowder, and Kesley thought he heard something like a grunt of pain, followed by a frantic threshing in the underbrush.

"I got him," a voice said.

"What of the other one?"

"We have him here."

"*Muy bien!* Don Miguel will be glad to see him."

Kesley was lifted to his feet. Dimly, he saw five men guarding him, and a sixth crouched a few feet away with his hand clapped to a raw knife-wound in his shoulder.

Efficiently, the bandits roped his arms to his sides. "I have a safe-conduct from Duke Miguel," Kesley protested, as they hustled him out of the copse.

One of the bandits snorted derisively. "Safe conduct? Pah! Don Miguel gives no safe conducts!"

"But —"

They were in the open now. There was no sign of van Alen or of van Alen's horse.

The six small ponies of the bandits' were grazing in a

wide circle; near the edge of the copse lay the two horses van Alen's blaster had brought down, and a few feet away were the sprawled, blackened corpses of the two dead bandits.

The night was silent. Even the birds had ceased their harsh noise. Kesley tensely allowed himself to be tethered to a pommel.

"Where are you taking me?" he demanded.

The bandit leader chuckled, showing a set of gleaming teeth. "Buenos Aires. The capital of Duke Miguel, no? Miguel is collecting *norteamericanos* this week!"

# THREE

AS WELL AS being the chief city of Argentina Province, Buenos Aires was a Ducal capital — the first such city Kesley remembered having entered.

He knew the names of the others: Chicago, Tunis, Johannesburg, Stockholm, Canberra, Strasbourg, Kiev, Hankow, Calcutta, Manila, Leopoldville. They were strange and alien names; to him, abstract symbols of Ducal power rather than concrete geographical localities.

It was easy to see that this was Miguel's abode. The walls of the city bristled with dark-skinned riflemen in blue shorts and gold brocade, zealously guarding their Immortal's city against armed attack. Standing outside the city walls, Kesley could see, looming above the blocks of low, grubby buildings, the arching sweep of Don Miguel's palace. A gleaming spire almost a hundred feet high topped the vaulted building, which looked down upon the nest of small houses clustered around it as a giant would upon worms.

There seemed to be a jam-up at the gates. Traffic was heavy at a Ducal capital. All around him, swarthy men on burros or horses or stubby piebald mutant beasts waited patiently to be admitted. Most of them were clad in broadbrimmed *sombreros* and colorful *serapes*; Kesley grinned wryly at that. South America was an unchanging microcosm. Beneath the friendly sky, life, frozen always in a stasis of todays, moved on slowly, with *manana* never quite arriving.

Kesley wondered about van Alen. The Antarctican had run away, and presumably had been shot by a bandit. Was he dead, his corpse lying rotting on the plain? It didn't matter, now. Kesley was in the hands of Duke Miguel. His destiny no longer bound to that of Dryle van Alen.

"Get along, now," a voice drawled. The line moved up. Slowly, the long queue was passing through the great double doors and into the city. Kesley's six captors surrounded him, three before and three aft. Their conversation during the long trip north to the capital had been limited to occasional rapid-fire bursts of incomprehensible Spanish, and Kesley still had no idea of the fate that awaited him.

"We go to the Duke," the taciturn leader said as they reached the gatekeeper. He gestured at Kesley. "We bring him a prize."

"*Norteamerico?*"

"*Si.*"

The gatekeeper flicked a thumb over his shoulder. "Go in."

Kesley's horse moved forward, and they entered the Ducal capital of Buenos Aires.

*Cities look pretty much alike*, Kesley thought, as

they entered. His short acquaintance with van Alen had made him more observant, more analytical. And, looking around, he framed the generalization. He might just as well have been in Galveston, or St. Louis.

There were differences, of course, but they were not fundamental ones. The dirt was a constant, the litter and the smell, and the undercurrent of noise. The crowds, too. And also the houses: squat, two- or three-story affairs, in the universally accepted architectural design, with gray whorls of greasy smoke spiralling up from their hearth fires.

Kesley wondered what cities had looked like in the Old Days, before the rain of bombs had leveled the world. New York had had millions of people in it. Buildings had towered to the skies. Kesley remembered how old Lester described a visit he had made to New York forty years earlier. The blistered hulks of the great towers still stood, jagged shells clawing at the sky. Forty, fifty, eighty stories high — it was unbelievable.

Cities were different now. The Twelve Dukes had laid down the unvarying pattern for the cities during the Time of Rebuilding, four hundred years before. The old names had been kept, and the old locations. But a city of the Twelve Empires now had a certain prescribed shape, and a city in Argentina Province looked much like one in Illinois Province, or Capetown Province. There was the wall, first of all, high and thick and protective. Within the wall, the radial spokes of streets, and the circling network of avenues, lined with low houses. At the heart of the city, the Building of Government or, as in Buenos Aires and eleven other cities in the world, the Ducal Palace.

Markets, shops, houses, schools, meeting-halls — these were all provided for, all according to plan.

"Why are you taking me to the Duke?" Kesley asked, as they trotted toward the towering palace.

The bandit chief shrugged. "The Duke wants *norteamericanos*. He pay us to bring them; he tell us where you and your friend are. We bring. See?"

Kesley nodded. It was the truth, he saw; the bandit had merely been following instructions.

*Everyone follows instructions*, he thought suddenly. He had followed van Alen's orders; the bandits were puppets of Don Miguel. And Miguel?

Who, he wondered, pulled the Duke's strings?

Kesley smiled. Van Alen had tainted him, with philosophy.

Life would undoubtedly have, been much simpler if he'd remained in Iowa Province, on the farm.

The contradiction followed at once: he *hadn't* been happy there, he realized. Life had never been simple — not even in a world where the benevolent Dukes tried manfully to avoid the fatal complexity of the Old Days.

They reached the approaches to the Palace, now. It was an imposing, almost breathtaking building. In seeing to it that the short-lived peoples of the world remained properly close to the ground, the Dukes had stressed their own grandeur. The milk-colored Palace swept upward like a bright fang piercing the sky. It was perhaps three blocks square at its base, and rushed upward for more than a hundred feet before its firm lines were broken by as much as a window.

The building's facade was frosty white and immaculate, a solid wall of irradiated polyethylene. Spotlights — even now, in the daytime — played against its shining bulk. The building was awesome, magnificent, a monolithic monument to a fortuitous mutation affecting but twelve men — and, thought Kesley, its very grandeur was faintly ridiculous.

A row of blue-clad guards was arrayed before the main entrance. Kesley's captors rode to the approach, and the bandit chief engaged in a brief colloquy, at the end of which one of the guards vanished within.

He returned a few moments later, bearing with him a small brown leather pouch. The bandit accepted the pouch eagerly, and tossed it to one of his men. *My price*, Kesley guessed in wry amusement. He was right. The bandit undid him and hauled him down from his mount. As Kesley gratefully flexed his numbed arms, the bandit shoved him toward the waiting guard.

"*Adios, norteamericano!*" The six bandits grinned cheerfully, pocketing their bounty. They remounted, and rode away.

"Come with me," the guard said stiffly. He drew a pistol, but Kesley shook his head.

"I won't make trouble. You can put that thing away." The great door swung open and Kesley was conducted into a vast courtyard lined with flowering shrubbery. At the far end of the yard, Kesley saw a small group of men standing in irregular formation.

"We go there," the guard said. He pointed, and Kesley started off in the direction indicated.

There were about ten men waiting there, under the surveillance of one of the Duke's guards, who watched them with drawn gun. As Kesley drew near, he saw that the men were, like himself, North Americans.

"Where are you from?" a white-haired man called. "Up north?"

"Iowa Province," Kesley said, joining the group. "You?"

"Illinois." The other's voice was bitter. "I'm from the court of Duke Winslow. He'll hear of this; he'll —"

The guard yelled:"Quiet down there!"

"What is all this?" Kesley whispered.

"I don't know. Miguel's evidently rounding up all the North Americans in his territory. It's illegal! It's —"

The guard whirled suddenly and struck the Illinois man across the face with his pistol. "Silence!"

Kesley felt a surge of anger, but restrained it. He bent and lifted the older man to his feet. Dazed, the courtier wiped blood from his tunic and dabbed gently at his gashed cheek. "Damn him," he muttered. He groped at his hip for a sword that wasn't there.

"Hush," Kesley said. "They'll only knock you down again. Fall in line and keep quiet. We'll find out what's going on later."

It was the only way to stay alive, he told himself. Fall in line; ask questions later.

Another door opened, and they entered the palace of the Duke.

"This way," the guard called. "After me." Shepherding them with his drawn pistol, he led the way, while three other guards closed in at each side of the group. Kesley looked around. They were in a long corridor which headed toward a descending staircase. The dungeons, obviously.

They kept walking. *Fall in line; ask questions later.* Kesley repeated it to himself.

Suddenly he stiffened. He had fallen obediently in line when van Alen had appeared from nowhere — and the questions that arose had never been answered. Now, perhaps, he was marching unquestioningly to his death. *I won't do it*, he thought defiantly, and stepped out of line.

He yanked the pistol from the astonished guard near him and slid his hand around the thick butt. The gun had an unfamiliar feel to it; it was heavy and clumsy. But be raised it quickly to shoulder-level and fired.

The guard at the front of the line yawped and clutched his shoulder. Kesley fired again. A second guard dropped. The other men in the line caught on, now, and charged the remaining pair of surprised guards. Kesley heard a pistol crack, and saw that it was in the hands of a North American.

*This* was the way. Act; instead of being acted upon.

Guards were coming down the corridor now, waving pistols. "Over here," Kesley yelled. He started to run back the way he had come. Turning the corridor, he collided with a surprised-looking fat man in reddish velvet robes, who had been moving forward in stately fashion, oblivious to the conflict ahead of him.

Kesley knocked the fat man off his legs and kept running. Behind him came the sounds of pistol shots echoing down the hall and the clatter of feet. Guards were coming from all over. He turned, fired three more times, and threw the useless gun away.

Four guards dashed toward him and, quickly, he backed into a dark alcove. There was a door. Impulsively, he threw it open and stepped inside.

A fist rocked him almost before he had crossed the threshold. Dizzily, Kesley wobbled backward to get a view of his assailant.

He was a big, broad-shouldered, black-bearded man wearing embroidered robes and a shining gold tiara. *A noble*, Kesley decided. *He packs a mean punch.*

The big man reached upward and yanked on a bell. Almost instantly, the room was full of guards. Determined to do as much damage as he could before being retaken, Kesley sprang forward. He clawed at the embroidered gold robes, feeling gold inlay ripping away under his fingernails. Then the noble hit him again, sending him staggering up against the wall. Two guards seized him.

"One of the escaped prisoners, *senor*," a guard

babbled. "How he got in here we do not know. He —"

"Enough, *payaso*. Take him away. Kill him."

A tired frown crossed the big man's forehead. "No. Forget that. Tie him to a chair, and leave him alone here with me."

The guard looked up doubtfully, but quickly concealed his misgivings. "Of course, sire."

"Send in my clothier also. This idiot has ruined my robes."

Kesley allowed himself to be tied to a chair.

"You're a bold fool," the big man said, coming over to glower down at Kesley. He knotted his fingers in his thick, tangled dark beard, and smiled, baring stained yellow teeth. Kesley met the noble's gaze evenly.

The deep eyes were set in a network of fine wrinkles. They were not the eyes of an ordinary man. They were heavy with the shadow of a hundred thousand days gone by, and infinities of days to come. Kesley realized that the man before him was no mere noble. He could only be Don Miguel, Duke of South America.

An Immortal.

# FOUR

KESLEY watched Miguel pace uneasily back and forth. The room he had blundered into was evidently one of the Ducal offices; a broad desk at the back was littered with a great many official-looking papers, and on one wall hung a glossy shield bearing Miguel's coat of arms.

Suddenly Miguel turned. "Where are you from?" he asked. His voice was deep, resonant, commanding.

"Iowa Province. I was a farmer."

"Oh? Then what might you be doing in my lands?"

Kesley saw that he had blundered. Farmers, normally, did not take pleasure jaunts to South America. He tried to repair the damage. "I was on a buying tour. I was down here for cattle, and grain, and —"

Miguel chuckled. "Enough, please. One does not have to be an Immortal to see through your lies." He pulled out a chair and sprawled his big form down. Smiling strangely, be said, "You can speak the truth. Why are you here?"

"I — I —" Kesley's face reddened. He realized that he had no rational answer to give. He was here only because van Alen had led him here — and van Alen was dead or wounded now, far to the south.

Miguel sighed. "You assassins are all alike. At the

moment of capture, you lose the sacred fire." Swiftly he leaned over and undid Kesley's bonds.

"There. You are free. Kill me, now. We're alone; this is your chance!"

Miguel slipped an ornamented stiletto from his sash and handed it to Kesley. Opening his cloak, the Duke fumbled with buttons and pulled the cloth aside, baring a broad, muscular chest covered with graying hair. "Here! Plunge the dagger in — *now!*"

Kesley weighed the stiletto in his hand, balancing the haft on his palm, fingering the weapon's keen point and well-honed blade. Miguel waited patiently. One corner of the Duke's wide mouth was drawn up in a cold smile; the other sagged almost uncontrollably into a drooping sneer.

"Well?"

Kesley feinted with the stiletto and flicked it through the air past Miguel's head and into the center of the arms-bearing shield on the wall. The Duke, who had not so much as blinked, laughed heartily.

"A good man with a knife! A good man indeed." Serious again, he said, "But you could have killed me. Why didn't you?"

"Kill an Immortal?" Kesley replied listlessly. "I'd sooner try to harness a whirlwind. How could I possibly kill you?"

"By plunging the knife into my heart," Miguel said. "You obviously fail to understand the true nature of our immortality."

"Which is?"

"Cell regeneration. Gradual rebuilding and replacement of decayed cells. We remain as we are because the decays of age are counteracted as rapidly as they occur. There are no organic defects to plague us. This process, however, does not guard against a knife in the heart, Or a slit throat, or a bullet in the back."

"And yet you gave the knife to me. Why?"

"I knew you wouldn't use it," Miguel said. "You short-lived ones are so terribly easy to understand. Only . . ."

The Duke's voice trailed off. "Only *what?*" Kesley prodded after a moment.

"Only nothing," Miguel said. He rose. "Come upstairs with me, young one, to my office. I am a slave to my duties . . . more thoroughly enslaved than the basest serf on my lands."

Miguel touched a panel in the wall and it slid back, revealing what looked to Kesley like an adjoining room.

"My private elevator," Miguel explained. "Come."

The elevator rose silently. When it stopped, the door slid open and Kesley found himself in an even vaster room, almost completely lined with books on one wall from floor to ceiling. Another wall was bright with paintings; on a third, strange lights flickered on a wide board, and glowing above their multicolored glitter were eight rectangular gray screens.

Seeming to forget Kesley, Miguel strode across the room and seated himself in an imposing chair facing the screens. He covered the flashing red light with his palm. The uppermost of the screens became illuminated. Kesley gasped as the face of a man grew visible.

The man in the green gesticulated humbly. "Your blessing, sire. Mendoza of Quito reporting, Don Miguel."

"Speak, Mendoza." Miguel's tone was regally impatient.

"It has not rained here for sixteen days, sire," Mendoza said anxiously. "The people are discontented. Crops are dying, and —"

"Enough." Miguel flipped a switch and a second screen came to life. "Luis, take care of this fool from Quito, and explain to him that we have no control over the weather. Then transfer all these other calls to your own line. I'll be busy for the next fifteen minutes."

The screen went blank; the flickering lights died away.

"What is that thing?" Kesley asked.

"Closed-screen television. I use it to keep in contact with my governors in the various provinces."

Miguel took a seat behind a desk; this one, like the other downstairs, heaped high with papers. He lowered his great, bearlike head between his hands and stared at Kesley for what must have been more than a minute. Finally he said, "I offered you a chance to kill me. You declined it."

"Perhaps if I got the chance again, I'd act differently," Kesley said.

"Perhaps. But the chance comes but once. I am not yet tired of life . . . I think." The Duke's eyes drooped wearily. They seemed to be staring backward into yesterday — and ahead at the burden of an endless tomorrow. "Four hundred years is many years, though. Are you married, young man?"

Startled, Kesley said: "Huh — no. No, not yet."

"I have been married thirty-six — no, forty-one times. The longest was the first: twenty-six years. We were both thirty when we met. When she died, she was fifty-six; I was still thirty. I was just finding out, then."

Miguel toyed with a sparkling, many-faceted gem on his desk.

"Most of the other marriages were short ones. . . . I couldn't bear to watch them grow old. Now I do not marry at all."

"Do you have children?" Kesley asked.

Miguel flinched as if struck. His wide lips tightened in anger; then his face softened again. "The gene is recessive," he said quietly. "And lethal in early childhood, if not immediately after birth. My dynasties have been short-lived. I have had eight children; seven lived less than a year. The eighth reached the age of nine."

He laughed hollowly. "Out of eternal life, nothing but death. No, I have no children, young one."

"I — see," Kesley said. He peered closely at the Immortal, feeling a strange flow of pity for the timeless man. Immortality was a costly gift, he saw. Suddenly, Kesley wondered how many other Immortals there had been beside the Twelve — Immortals who, once they realized the terrible nature of their breed, had taken their own lives. More than one, he thought.

And how often did Miguel himself consider suicide? Had he had some hidden protection against Kesley's knife, moments ago downstairs, or had the Duke been half-hoping the blade would strike true?

Perhaps.

"Why do you keep me here?" Kesley asked.

Miguel looked up slowly. His eyes, deep and piercing, bored into Kesley's. "You amuse me," Miguel said. "When one is more than four centuries old, one is hard put to find amusement. I am amused by the possibility that you might strike me dead at any moment."

"It's really very funny," Kesley said.

"I'm amused by the fact that you're not afraid of me. Awed, yes, but not servile. How many times a day do you think I hear that hateful word 'Sire'? *Sire!* Me, who has sired eight dead babes and nothing more."

Kesley looked away, embarrassed. "Sire also means ruler," he pointed out in a muffled voice.

"That, too," Miguel said. "I rule, and it is my life to rule. I have ruled four hundred years, and I will rule four thousand more — or four thousand thousand, or four million. But I can never stop ruling. It is a burden I can never put down. Who would fill the vacuum I would leave?"

"There were rulers before the Twelve Dukes."

"And they destroyed the world! Destroyed it — and

in so doing, brought us into being. No, stranger, my Dukedom I can never put down. But it wearies me to make always the petty decisions, to govern the lives of petty —"

"Why are you telling me all this?" Kesley burst out.

"Mere amusement," Miguel said evenly. "I enjoy talking to you. What is your name?"

"Dale Kesley."

"Dale Kesley," Miguel repeated. "A fine North American name, square-cut and undistinguished. I like it."

The Duke gestured toward a communicator-tube on his desk. "Bring that to me."

Shrugging, Kesley handed him the tube. Miguel switched it on. "Send Archbishop Santana here at once," he barked, and cut the channel.

He glanced at Kesley. "The Archbishop will swear you to my service, Dale Kesley."

"But I'm a vassal of Duke Winslow," Kesley protested.

Miguel chuckled heartily. "A vassal of Duke Winslow," he mimicked. "Vassal, indeed. You turn down my offer? You throw Duke Winslow in my face?"

"An oath is an oath, Don Miguel."

"Oaths? Who are you to talk of oaths? You're nothing but a paid assassin — don't think I haven't overlooked that."

Kesley started to protest, but saw there was nothing to be gained by arguing. Miguel would never believe him.

"His Holiness Archbishop Santana," the wall-announcer said.

The door slid open and the Archbishop entered. As the plump figure waddled into the room, Kesley grinned in recognition. The Archbishop was the fat man in velvet robes whom he had bowled over in his mad flight downstairs.

Now the priest wore a simple black surplice and mitred hat and carried the crook symbolic of his office. He was a small, rotund man with dark olive skin and a thin, sharply-hooked nose that seemed highly misplaced in his otherwise plumply rounded countenance. He paused at the door, smiling benignly, and made the sign of the cross with two swift motions in the air.

"Come on in, Santana," Miguel ordered.

The priest approached Miguel and bowed deeply, then glanced at Kesley. Suspicion was evident on his smoothly-shaven face.

"This is Dale Kesley of North America," Miguel said.

"We have met," the priest said unctuously. "This young man knocked me down while fleeing from your guards, sire."

Kesley grinned imperceptibly, catching Miguel's faint, involuntary wince at the *sire*. "It was an accident, Father. I was fleeing hastily; I didn't see you."

"Time wastes," Miguel said. "Santana, swear this young man quickly into my service. I have work for him."

The priest began to raise his crook, but Kesley shook his head. "No, Don Miguel. I told you I'm a vassal of Duke Winslow."

Miguel smiled. "But Duke Winslow's oath is no longer binding upon his vassals, you know."

"I didn't know. When did this happen?"

"It hasn't, yet. But it will shortly — when Duke Winslow is assassinated."

"But — when —"

"Soon," Miguel said. His cold smile was painful to watch. "And your hand," the Immortal continued, "will be the one that strikes him down."

"You're crazy," Kesley said shortly.

Miguel paled, and Santana crossed himself rapidly several times.

"You don't talk like that to your Duke," the Archbishop said.

"*My* Duke? But —"

Don Miguel regained his composure and put one hand on Kesley's shoulder. "I ask you to join me and perform this service. I am prepared to pay well for it."

"The price?"

"My daughter," Miguel said. "Kill Winslow, and she's yours."

"Your *daughter?* But I thought —"

"*Adopted* daughter," Miguel said smoothly. "My ward. The girl is but twenty-two, and lovely. Kill Winslow, and she's yours."

Kesley felt perspiration dripping down his body. Kill

Duke Winslow? Upset the balance of the Twelve Empires, break the fragile harmony on which the world depended? It was impossible!

But —

He realized suddenly that he was a totally free agent, detached and uninvolved. Van Alen had led him forth from Iowa Province, and van Alen was dead. He owed nothing to van Alen, nothing to Iowa.

He stood alone, unknown and unwanted in the world of the Twelve Empires, able to shape his own destinies. And Miguel was offering him a title, a home, an allegiance, at the cost of an assassination.

*Well, why not?* he asked himself. *My hand is free. Why not strike down a Duke?*

He moistened his lips. "I'll consider it," he said. "But first — let me see the girl."


Alone, waiting for Miguel to return, Kesley tried to think.

Kill Winslow?

Kill a Duke — an Immortal?

The idea seemed incredible, almost obscene. It was like saying, "Snuff out a star," or, "Destroy a world." The Dukes were centers of their universes, and one did not kill them.

Yet —

Kesley's self-searching in the past few minutes had revealed one jarring fact: he did not have the qualms he had supposed he would have. Assassinating Winslow would not be star-snuffing; he knew he could do it as casually as van Alen had blasted the blue wolf, back in Iowa Province.

He knew he should be quaking at the thought of murdering his own Duke, but the necessary quaking refused to come.

*What's wrong with me?* he asked himself desperately. *Why am I different?*

A man was supposed to feel loyalty to his Duke. Kesley did not. *Why?*

He had had a chance to kill Miguel. Perhaps that had all been illusion; perhaps he would have been struck down by an invisible guard the moment the knife's tip approached the Immortal's flesh. Perhaps not. He had drawn back, only because he had nothing to gain by killing the Duke.

And now he was asked to kill another. *Dale Kesley, Hired Assassin. We Kill Dukes.* He grinned mirthlessly.

The faint hum of the sliding panel sounded behind him. He turned.

"Have you reached any decision yet?" Miguel asked, stepping into the room.

"You know what I'm waiting to see," Kesley said.

"Of course."

Miguel beckoned to someone standing beyond the panel. "My daughter," he said to Kesley. "The Lady Narella."

No one appeared. Miguel scowled and reached through the open panel. He yanked — and the Lady Narella appeared.

"Oh," Kesley said.

Narella was quite a woman.

She stood with her hands on her hips, smoky, violet-hued eyes blazing in defiance of Kesley and even of Miguel. She was making it clear that she was no one's pawn, not to be bandied about.

Narella wore an ermine wrap, and a low-cut tunic that clung tightly to her high breasts and lean form. She was a tall girl with wide hips and shoulders. Dark hair fell loosely about her face; she wore the diamond-encrusted tiara of a Ducal Princess, and her full lips were bright with a fluorescing cosmetic of some sort. Here and there — on her forehead above the left eyebrow, on her right cheek, on the creamy flesh where the base of her throat swelled into rising breasts — she wore a scintillating dab of brightness, a dot of some chemical that glittered radiantly from its own inner light.

Kesley had never seen a royal woman before. Strangely, or not so strangely, he felt all the reverence for her that he had failed to feel in the presence of the Immortal alone. Had Miguel not been there, he probably would have knelt despite himself and begged to kiss the tip of her cloak.

"Is this the man, sire?" she asked. Her voice was a fit complement to her body, deep and warm, throbbing and throaty.

"It is," Miguel said. "Dale Kesley — the Lady Narella."

"Hello," she said coldly.

A muscle quivered in Kesley's cheek. He nodded curtly to the girl. "Hello."

She ignored him and turned to Miguel. "Is this the man to whom you're selling me, sire?"

Miguel grimaced. "You wound me, girl. I'll leave the two of you together to talk."

"No!" she said imperiously, but it was too late. Miguel, with an enigmatic smile, had bowed and stepped backward into the waiting elevator. The panel slid shut. The wall was once again unbroken.

Slowly, she turned to face Kesley. "I won't have any part of this! I don't belong to Miguel! He can't give me away like this — to a *commoner*!"

Kesley smiled. "Your nostrils flare very nicely when you're angry, milady."

She whirled and stalked across the room, where she stood, her back to him. Kesley grinned amiably. This display of temper was enjoyable. The girl had spirit. Kesley liked that.

"Miguel called you his *daughter*," he said loudly. "How come? That's impossible, of course."

"How do you know?" she snapped, turning to face him. Her dark eyes glittered angrily. "I'm Miguel's daughter. Who says I'm not?"

"Miguel. He told me you were adopted. He told me Immortals were sterile, that their children didn't survive. Whose daughter are you?"

"What is it to you?"

Kesley shrugged. "Curiosity, I guess. You're quite

lovely, you know."

She said nothing.

"You're supposed to thank people when they compliment you, milady. It's hardly polite to —"

"Quiet!" She crossed the room and faced him across a desk. At close range her faint perfume reached Kesley's nostrils; it was a delightful odor. The violet of her eyes, he saw, was flecked lightly with gold. "Why has Miguel promised me to you?"

"He wants me to carry out a job — an assassination. You're the price."

"Blunt, aren't you?"

"Would you rather have me lie?"

"No," she said, after a moment's thought. She threw back her shoulders and glared defiantly. at him. "Well, do I pass your inspection? Am I fit for you?"

Kesley made no answer. Instead, he circled deftly around the desk, drew her close, pulled her mouth up to his. He kissed her warmly without eliciting any response. She remained passive in his arms, as if she were a particularly lovely statue rather than a living woman.

He released her.

"Are you through?" she asked acidly.

"You pass the test," he said. Then he shook his head tiredly. "No. This is insane. Narella, who are you?"

Apparently his sudden sincerity, after the romantic pretense of the minutes before, told upon her. "My father was a court singer in Chicago, court poet to Duke Winslow. I was raised at the court. Four years ago, my father disappeared. Then Duke Winslow gave me to Miguel as a wife, but Miguel didn't want any wives. He adopted me instead. I've lived here ever since, as his daughter. As for my father, I suppose he's dead. He was blind, and —"

"*Blind?*" Kesley snapped instantly out of his mood of weariness as if a bolt of electricity had seared through him. "Did you say your father was a blind court singer?"

"Yes," she said.

Words came from nowhere and rumbled in Kesley's mind, words spoken on an Iowa farm in the deep, booming voice of van Alen the Antarctican:

*"We have the treasure, now; we lack only the key to the box. Daveen the Singer, the blind man. The search for him continues."*

Slowly Kesley raised his head. He blinked a little as his eyes encountered the flashing glitter of the girl's jewelry; then he looked at her eyes and at the lips whose cosmetic fluorescence remained in neat array despite his kiss. "Your father's name — was it Daveen?"

"Yes," she said. "Yes! But how do you know?"

"I don't. It's a name I've heard mentioned, a name that has something to do with me. Only . . . have you ever seen me before?"

"I think so," she said slowly. "But I don't remember it. Were you ever at the court of Duke Winslow?"

"Never. But I recall you from somewhere. I —"

Dizzily, he looked away as a burst of sudden pain flooded his mind. He shuddered and felt sick.

"What's the matter?" she asked anxiously.

"I — don't know."

"You look ill. You've gone completely pale." She put her arms around him as if to steady him, and her warmth sustained him through the moment of terror that had overtaken him. It was as if he had struck some particularly sensitive nerve, and the resonances were carrying agony through his body.

When it was over, he mopped the beads of cold sweat from his forehead. He looked up at her and saw that her glacial remoteness had been replaced by a sort of feminine warmth, almost a maternal solicitude.

"Would you like to find your father again?" he asked in a low voice.

She nodded.

"So would I. I don't know why, but I feel Daveen holds the key to the hidden areas of my life, the inconsistencies. I'd like to find him for myself. And for you."

"Would you?"

"First ask, *could you?* Your father may be dead, for all I know." He took her hand. "Narella — you don't want to stay here with Miguel?"

"No," she said.

"Good. Listen carefully. Does Miguel have big ears?"

She frowned. "I don't understand."

"Never mind. Come here."

She came close and he pulled her up against him. This time her lips rose willingly for the kiss, but he brushed her pale cheek instead and let his mouth graze lightly along her face until it reached the tip of her earlobe.

"Does Miguel have this room wired for sound?" he whispered. "Can he hear what we say?"

She nodded almost imperceptibly. "Probably," she whispered back.

"That's what I thought. Stay close to me, then, and hear what I have to say. If he's watching he'll think we're making love."

"Go ahead," she said.

"I'm going to accept Miguel's commission and leave here to assassinate Duke Winslow, as ordered."

She gasped. "Assassinate —"

"That's the terms of our agreement," he said. "One Duke more or less doesn't matter to me. I'll go to Winslow's court and try to find out what happened to your father. Somehow I'll give Winslow what's due him. Then I'll return here and claim you as Miguel's agreed, and we'll go looking for your father together. If you're willing, give me a kiss."

She hesitated for just a moment, then lifted his face from her ear. Their eyes met. She was pale, he saw, and frightened; the aloof haughtiness of the court lady had been almost completely replaced by an appealing little-girl terror.

He looked past her to the brooding eyes of Don Miguel glowering down at him from the row of paintings on the wall. After *Winslow — Miguel*, he thought with sudden savagery. The unprovoked thought surprised him.

"Very well," she murmured. She touched her lips lightly to his, and then gave herself to him with a sort of desperate abandon that astonished Kesley.

After a moment or two, he slipped from her grasp and looked around the room, wondering if he'd find a concealed television camera or something similar. There was nothing. The battery of screens and lights on the far wall seemed dead, as they had been since Miguel had shut them off.

Finally he cupped his hands. "Miguel!"

The Duke reappeared almost instantly, followed closely by the chubby form of Archbishop Santana. The Archbishop once again performed the sign of the cross piously as he entered.

"Well?" Miguel asked.

"State your terms once again," said Kesley.

Miguel frowned. "The room is crowded."

"I know, sire. Witnesses may be in order."

"Very well," Miguel said wearily. "In return for services to be rendered, I do promise the hand of my ward, the Lady Narella, to Dale Kesley of my vassalage."

"When?"

"Upon his return from the successful completion of his endeavors in my behalf."

"Said endeavors being?" Kesley prodded mercilessly.

"The elimination of Duke Winslow of North America," Miguel said. "His death by any means whatsoever."

"All right," Kesley said. He glanced from Miguel to the Archbishop — who seemed somewhat pale beneath his olive skin — to Narella. "Now that terms have been stated, we can talk business; Miguel, what assurance do I have that I'll get the girl when I come back?"

"An Immortal is good to his word," the Duke said gruffly. "You have a witness in the person of the Archbishop."

"Surely you will not require the Duke to swear an oath?" Santana exclaimed in a shocked voice. "My presence will certify — as if certification were necessary — that —"

"Enough, padre," Kesley said. There was nothing to be won by forcing Miguel into an oath; he had already given his word as an Immortal, and if he would break that, it was reasonable to suspect that no other oath would bind him.

He looked at the girl again. *Daveen's daughter*, he thought. He wondered what tangled relationship of cause and effect had brought him to this place at this time, and where van Alen, who had set the whole chain of events in motion, was now.

In a month's time Kesley had been transformed from an ignorant Iowa farmer into a killer of Dukes and a wooer of noble ladies. It was a strange progress, but it was hopeless, Kesley thought, to try to account for the vagaries of fate.

"Will you accept and enter my vassalage?" Miguel asked.

Kesley met the Immortal's gaze squarely and this time, and this time it seemed to him, it was those dark, four-hundred-year-old eyes that gave ground instead of his own.

"I accept," he said.

He forced himself to kneel and kiss the golden hem of Don Miguel's jeweled cloak.

# FIVE

THE DUCAL capital of Chicago sprawled in a lazy ring on the banks of Lake Michigan, in Illinois Province. As Dale Kesley and his small retinue waited outside the city's walls before requesting admission, the thought occurred to him once again that the world's cities were similar. As he looked at Chicago, it seemed to him that he might never really have left Buenòs Aires.

Duke Winslow's palace, visible high in the background overlooking the calm lake, might have been an exact replica of Don Miguel's, except that its flat walls were hewn from broad slabs of flesh-red feldspar instead of spun, as Miguel's were, from shimmering polyethylene. In the stagnant, late-August air, the sun's rays hit the palace walls weakly, giving them an oily glare that Kelsey found displeasing. But still he preferred the natural blockiness of the stone to the consistent slickness of the plastic that formed the walls of Miguel's palace. Polyethylene walls were the products of controlled hard radiation and, controlled or no, Kesley, like all men, found the concept of radiation repugnant. It jarred against ingrained taboos.

His eye, becoming city-familiar now, began to detect other differences between Winslow's capital and Miguel's.

The guards posted in Chicago's outer walls lacked the tense urgency of the small brown men who protected Buenos Aires; they stared outward with a sleepy complacency that seemed to characterize the entire city and possibly, Kesley admitted, the entire North American Empire. Here in the north, there was none of the crackling atmosphere of tension that seemed to prevail in Buenos Aires.

Kesley's horse, a firm-fleshed black thoroughbred of the Old Kind, furnished by Miguel and transported with finicking care from South America, pawed impatiently at the layer of fine ash that covered the ground outside the city, and snorted. Kesley steadied the animal with soothing pressures of his calves and thighs; the horse detected the signals and subsided.

"Shall we go in?" Kesley asked.

"Why not?" came the reply from his left. Kesley glanced over at the rider, Archbishop Santana. "We are here, and the time is proper," the priest said.

Kesley turned in the saddle to gesture at his six men. They rode behind at a respectful distance, six well-muscled members of Miguel's guard, resplendent in their imperial blue shorts and flashing yellow jackets. Kesley urged his horse forward; Santana, a surprisingly good horseman despite his unathletic physique, did the same, and the six guards followed. They advanced to the wall.

A toll-keeper waited there, a dried old man in Ducal uniform seated beside an immense tollbox ornamented with Duke Winslow's arms. Kesley reined in before him and drew out a jangling leather pouch.

The toll-keeper's lips moved silently as he counted the party. "Eight dollars," he said.

*"For cierto."* Kesley leaned far to the right and handed the man the pouch.

"Eight dollars of that is for toll, *amigo.*"

Frowning, the old man undid the drawstrings, emptying the contents of the pouch into his wrinkled palm. Eight tiny golden dollars rolled out, followed by a massive imperial doubloon of Miguel's coinage. A faint blink was the only acknowledgement the toll-keeper showed; nodding curtly, he dropped the eight dollars in the till, pocketed the doubloon as if by divine right, and gestured casually within with a quick toss of his head.

As Kesley and his party proceeded through the heavy gate, Kelsey grinned quietly to himself. He wished van Alen could have seen the strange metamorphosis of his one-time protege: here he was, clad in the lustrous velvet robes of a Knight of the Empire of South America, riding a full-blooded, spirited, Old-Kind horse instead of a swaybacked, scaly old mutant, and distributing largesse with the natural air of the high-born.

He entered the city proper at a slow canter, the Archbishop at his side, his men behind. The streets were crowded. Chicago, built on the very ashes of the old City of that name, was the largest city of Duke Winslow's territories, home to some three hundred thousand souls. Kelsey saw eyes brighten at the sight of his magnificent horse; men in the streets cleared back, giving way, as the South American party entered.

"We should find an inn first of all," the Archbishop advised. "Tomorrow, you and I will try to seek audience with the Duke."

Kesley shook his head. "We announce ourselves to the Duke at once; we tell him we'll have an audience tomorrow. None of this begging for an appointment.

Santana shrugged. "As you wish, *Señor Ramon*." The sudden, hard, sardonic inflection in the Archbishop's purring voice mocked the false title Miguel had bestowed on Kelsey for the purpose of the journey.

Kesley rode silently on, brooding over his mission. He had agreed lightly enough, back in Buenos Aries, to the assassination of Winslow, but now that he actually was in Winslow's own capital, with the rosy bulk of the Ducal Palace towering ahead, he wondered how he could have acceded so casually to so dangerous and so terrible a mission.

The looming palace ahead was the nerve-center of a continent, and one man — *one man* — controlled the multitude of ganglia. The entire vast spread of North America, from the dismal radiation-roasted Eastern seaboard to the broad plains of the Middle-West farming country to the open, relatively unscathed lands of the far West, depended for its organization on Chicago and on Chicago's Duke.

For the first time, Kesley realized the immensity of the confusion that would result when he struck down

Winslow. He had no motive for the crime, either; it would be a sheerly gratuitous act, performed as a gesture of disengagement and nothing more.

But what could Miguel's motive in upsetting the balance of the world possibly be? Surely, Kesley thought, the South American Duke knew what would happen once Winslow was removed. The taut framework of North American life would collapse inward on itself like a puffball that had discharged its dusty cloud of spores.

Who would profit? Miguel? Were assassins now drawing near the Ducal Palaces of Stockholm, of Johannesburg, of Canberra, readying themselves to rid the world of all Dukes but Miguel at one bold stroke? If so, why? Did Miguel want the crushing responsibility of the entire globe's governance strapped to his shoulders for all eternity?

It seemed unlikely. Kesley thought of the Immortal's deep, weary eyes, and of the moment of weakness when Miguel had let his heavy head sink between his hands. No, Miguel had some other motive.

Amusement, perhaps.

Kesley nodded. That was it: amusement. Having long since exhausted the pleasures of his power, having tasted everything human life had to offer, the timeless man was searching desperately for a relief from boredom.

For that reason he had bared his chest to Kesley's knife and, perhaps, he had not cared whether Kesley struck or not. For the same reason, he had chosen Kesley at random to remove Winslow, to upset the balance, to *change things*.

Kesley shuddered. What a nightmare an Immortal's life must be, he thought, once the first few centuries had passed.

Later, Kesley rode back from the palace with a little less lordliness than he had had going forth.

"That major-domo had nerve," he remarked mournfully, as the little band of South Americans trotted through the broad palace approaches toward the gate leading back into the city. "An appointment next week! Who does Winslow think he is? And what does he think of Miguel, if he treats his ambassadors this way?"

"Peace, son," the Archbishop said. "Be philosophical. Duke Winslow is a busy man and a proud one. I warned you this would happen."

"But we're *ambassadors!*"

"Exactly so. Had we been ragamuffins we would have had a better chance of an immediate audience." Santana shook his head. "You fail to see that Winslow is deliberately humbling us to stress his own superiority over Miguel."

"I hadn't thought of it that way," Kesley admitted. "Of course. He was just telling us to stand outside and wait around until he was ready to let us kiss the Ducal robe."

"Precisely. And our course now is simple. We find

lodging, and we allow a week to pass. Then, Winslow will see us. And then, my friend, the time will come for you to carry out our Duke's command."

"I know."

Kesley felt himself perspiring heavily beneath his ambassadorial robes, and not entirely because of the humid air. He knew — and Santana as well, evidently — that he had no plan for slaying Winslow. He was counting on some random twitch of the Immortal's psychology to put the Duke in his power. But would Winslow, as had Miguel, bare his chest willingly to the blade?

Probably not, Kesley thought balefully. From what he had already deduced of the workings of the Immortal mind, it was hardly likely that any two Dukes would share a behavioral pattern. And that left Kesley in an awkward position.

"A week is a long time," Kesley said, as they rode through the gates. The double doors clanged shut behind them, sealing off Winslow's palace from the city. "I'll be ready when the time comes, padre."

"I hope so. I will pray for your soul," the priest intoned.

"Fine," Kesley said savagely. "Pray for me sincerely, father. *Pater noster* —"

"Don't mock what you don't understand," Santana said. He crossed himself fervently. "Your soul is in danger, *Señor* Ramon."

"*My* soul? What about yours, you old windbag?"

Santana squirmed in the saddle, faced Kesley. The

plump priest's sad eyes gazed mournfully into Kesley's. "My soul?" Santana repeated. "My soul is long since forfeit, but I pray constantly for my salvation."

Kesley reddened. "What do you mean by —"

He cut himself off in mid-sentence and pointed to the left. "What's *that*?" he asked hoarsely. "Mutant?"

"Yes," the Archbishop said. "There are many of them in Chicago. I think he plans to make trouble; be ready to defend yourself."

The creature was coming toward them out of a jumble of clumsily-thatched huts strung in a wobbly circle around a gullied heap of slag at the extreme left side of the road. It was tall — nearly seven feet, Kesley estimated — with elongated spidery limbs and a bloated, almost hydrocephaloid skull, devoid of hair. The mutant wore only a rag twisted carelessly about its middle; the body thus revealed was grotesquely piebald in color, blotched and spotted, the purpling skin lying loosely and peeling away in great leprous flakes.

Kesley had seen mutants before: mutant horses, mutant wolves, other products of ravaged genes, but he had never before been this close to a *human* sport, other than Miguel. Miguel was human in all physical aspects save his life span; the creature shambling toward them now could be called "human" only by the loosest of definitions.

As the mutant approached, a musty odor of decay drifted before him. Kesley shuddered involuntarily.

Once, he knew, the cities of the world had been populated by almost as many mutants as normals. That had been in the days immediately after the great blast, before the Dukes had taken command of the world.

But most of these mutants had been sterile, carrying, like the Dukes, lethal genes. Others carried recessive characteristics only. Gradually, through the centuries, the mutant population had died out and dwindled away into scattered groups here and there in the biggest cities — and, word was, there was one city somewhere in Illinois populated only by mutants.

This one was blind, Kesley saw now, but it moved with unerring accuracy.

"Archbishop Santana!" the creature called, in a hoarse croak of a voice. "Wait for me, Archbishop!"

"How does he know you?" Kesley asked.

"Some of them have strange powers," Santana whispered. He nervously undid the crucifix that hung from the breast of his surplice and held it before him, as if to ward off the Devil.

The mutant merely chuckled. "Put away your toy, Archbishop. I don't frighten so easily."

"Stay back," Kesley snapped. "Keep away from us." To Santana he said, "Let's get out of here. Spur your horse and let's go."

"No. Let's hear him out."

The mutant stationed himself directly in their path and pointed a twisted, lumpy forefinger at Santana. "Behold the man of God," he croaked. *"Ecce homo!"*

"What do you want?" the Archbishop demanded.

Kesley saw that Santana was sheet-white beneath his outward duskiness.

"I want nothing. I merely came out here to laugh at the Archbishop of God who has come to Chicago on a mission of *murder!*"

Kesley stiffened in the saddle, but Santana caught his arm just as he was about to go for his gun. "What is this talk of murder?" Santana demanded.

Late afternoon clouds were dropping over the city now, and a cool wind came sweeping in from the lake. Kesley shivered as the mutant grinned, baring scraggly stumps of yellow teeth.

"Murder? Did I say murder? But there will be no murder, milord. Merely betrayal — and betrayal again."

That night, in the rooms they had taken near the city's central marketplace, the image of the mutant haunted Kesley, imposing itself before his eyes with demonic insistence.

Betrayal? No murder? The paradoxes and cloaked ambiguities the grotesque creature had uttered ground into Kesley's already sensitive consciousness, bringing with them the sharp image of the piebald spider of a man that was the mutant.

Kesley looked across the room to Santana. The plump Archbishop, having divested himself of his traveling costume, wore a loose cassock without surplice. He was thumbing the pages of his breviary, flicking rapidly over matter long since committed to memory.

"Padre?"

"Eh?"

"That mutant this afternoon —"

"Don't speak of him," Santana said.

"But he bothers me, Santana. I can't get him out of my mind, him or that crazy nonsense he was muttering."

"That was not nonsense," the Archbishop said in a hollow voice. "He struck at the heart, that man."

"I don't understand."

"You yourself made the same comment earlier, when you remarked that I, a man of God, am with you to participate in this unholy mission. Why, you ask. You asked me if I were not risking my immortal soul by accompanying you."

"And you said —"

"I said that I had little to risk. Strange words, coming from an Archbishop, but my soul is long since forfeit. God works in strange ways, and so his servants follow."

"You're still talking in riddles," Kesley complained. "Why did you come along, then, if you knew it would damn you?"

"I am already *damned* for serving Miguel!" Santana cried. His doughy face was taut with sudden animation. "Don't you see that Miguel and his Dukes have overthrown Rome, have supplanted Christ with themselves? And we continue to serve them, not because we desire it, but because we must!"

Kesley frowned. A light of torment, almost of martyrdom, gleamed in the Archbishop's eyes now.

"What difference does it make," Santana asked, "if I help you kill Winslow? I cannot be any more damned than I am already — and possibly, possibly the consequences of your act will — will — do you see?"

"Killing Winslow will topple the whole apple cart," Kesley said softly. "You're gambling an already assured damnation against the chance that knocking off one Duke will crush all the rest and restore your religion to supremacy." He chuckled quietly. "I sometimes wonder just whose catspaw I am," he said.

"Everyone's," the priest remarked. "Poor pawn, you've fallen fair of everyone's scheming."

The priest continued to read for a while, then uttered a brief prayer in rapid Spanish — perhaps it was even Latin, Kesley thought — and blew out his candle. Kesley closed his eyes and tried to sleep.

Sleep would not come. Brooding, he rolled and fidgeted, seeing over and over again the loose-jointed, hideous figure of the mutant.

# Six

"I'LL BE BACK LATER," Kesley said in the morning. His eyes stung as if they had been sandpapered during the long, sleepless night; his lips were dry and cracking, and the oppressive city heat hung around him like the caress of a giant velvet glove, smothering without actually touching.

"Where are you going?" Santana asked, not looking up. It was a mechanical question asked out of mere courtesy, and Kesley ignored it.

"Saddle my horse," he told one of the men. "I won't need any of you to go with me."

The morning air was already steaming as he rode out into the city. The market was crowded with sleepy-eyed Chicagoans haggling for the fruit and vegetables that had been brought in while they slept. Kesley traversed the marketplace in a wide circuit and struck out along the broad cobbled road that led to Duke Winslow's palace.

About halfway there, he cut sharply and veered to the right, guiding his horse down a steep hill and off onto a narrow, red-brown unpaved road. Looking ahead, he could see his destination: the impossibly untidy bramble of shanties that was the ghetto of the mutants.

Even at this distance, he could see bizarre creatures moving idly back and forth down below, wandering from porch to porch in the isolated colony. He whitened at the sight of some of them.

There was one round, orange, doughy mass of a man that looked like some sort of giant fruit, except for the enlarged features and the tiny, stick-like legs and arms that projected from it; nearby, walking in confused circles, was a mutant with a pair of dissimilar writhing heads and an uncountable number of busy legs.

Lazy curlicues of smoke hung wavering in the air above the shacks. Kesley looked around.

*Great God*, he thought suddenly. *They're people!*

He rode down into the ghetto, feeling ashamed of his own bodily symmetry and genetic heritage, which seemed abnormal here. He, alone, of all the human beings within a half-mile radius, was untainted, and the thought made him feel strangely humble.

"Who is it you want?" a man asked. *The toll-keeper*, Kesley thought with sudden weird irony.

The "man" facing him was more nearly human than most; only a blob of flesh dangling from his forehead and a wattled reddish dewlap swinging pendulously below his chin qualified him for the ghetto. Kesley forced himself to stare rigidly over the man's shoulder while he replied.

"I'm looking for . . . I don't know his name. He's tall, very tall, and —" He broke off, overwhelmed by self-conscious guilt, unable to recite the catalogue of one mutant's alienness to another.

"Go ahead," the mutant said with surprising warmth. "Tell me what he looks like and I'll see if I can find him. I'm not offended."

Kesley licked his lips and proceeded to describe the man he sought as vividly as possible. When he was through, the mutant nodded.

"You look for Lomark Dawnspear, friend. Has he wronged you?"

"No," Kesley said hastily, beginning to wish he had never come. "I just want to talk to him."

"Wait here. I'll try to bring him to you."

Kesley waited. The mutant vanished in the confusing tangle of closely-packed shacks.

In the midst of this poverty and genetic horror, Kesley held himself perfectly still, hoping not to call to himself the attention of some unfortunate who might be jealous of his fine clothes or unscrambled chromosomes. But no one approached him. The mutants held their distance, eyeing him with unashamed curiosity from the cramped porches of their huts.

It was a panorama of total ghastliness. Kesley could see now where the horror with which men regarded the Old Days had arisen: the people here were living reminders of the crime of the Old World — a crime, Kesley thought, whose consequences were visited upon the tenth and the twentieth generations.

"You seek me?" a harsh voice said. Kesley snapped

to attention and saw the hoarse-voiced Jeremiah of the streets approaching him, escorted by the dewlapped one. Kesley nodded; this was the man. In such profusion of mutation, there would hardly be two so marked.

"Do you remember who I am?" Kesley asked.

The mutant chuckled. "Could I forget? You're the young killer from the southlands, up here to do away with — but hush! I must not give it away!"

Kesley gripped the mutant by the baggy folds of flesh that hung loosely on one spidery arm. "How do you know anything of who I am?"

The mutant shrugged. "How could I keep from knowing?" His voice was mild and apologetic now, with little of its earlier raucous quality. "I can no more keep from knowing, than you — than you can keep from needing food, or seeing when your eyes are open. I . . . *know.*"

"How much do you know?"

"Why you are here, and where you are from . . . and where you will go, and what you will become." Lomark Dawnspear's voice had modulated into a dull, almost ritualistic drone. "I see these things, and I do not speak. I speak, but you do not see. Blind, I know you. Eyes open, you march into treachery."

Kesley released the mutant and stepped back. He was shaking with inward horror; his empty stomach seemed to be squirming. "What are you talking about?"

The mutant smiled feebly. "Counter-question: who is your father, handsome blond man?"

"My father? I —"

"You do not know?"

"All right — I don't know. Do you?"

"How could I not know? Can the maggot restrain its hunger? Can the Earth forget its orbit?"

"You know, but you're not talking. Is that it?"

Dawnspear shrugged again. "You would not want me to tell you," he said softly. "I see that, too."

"All right," Kesley said, irritated. "Forget all about that. Give me some other answers."

"If I can."

"The man named van Alen — is he dead?"

"No."

"Where is he?"

"In his home. Antarctica."

"It was true, then," Kesley said. He stated into the mutant's dead eyes. "Who is he?"

"A noble of the Antarctican land," Lomark Dawn-spear said. "Forget van Alen. Watch Miguel . . . and Winslow. Watch everyone, youngster. Watch Santana, the greasy prelate. Watch me. Watch the fool stealing up behind you this very minute."

"The oldest trick in the world," Kesley said skeptically. But he felt a sudden cold sensation between his shoulderblades, and whirled quickly. Another mutant stood there, a wide, slablike thing with four arms pivoting off jointed shoulders. One of its thick-fingered hands clutched a rock, jagged and heavy.

Moving instinctively Kesley grasped the arm holding the rock and yanked it down, smashing a fist into the broad creature's stomach at the same time. The rock thudded to the ground; the four arms windmilled aimlessly for a moment or two, and then the mutant backed off mumbling stertorous, incomprehensible curses.

"You'd better leave," Lomark Dawnspear said, "Some of the slower ones are beginning to realize you're here. They're likely to make things dangerous for you."

"But you haven't told me a thing," Kesley said.

"The answers lie ahead of you . . . the answers and the questions. Now go."

Scowling, Kesley drew his robe tighter around his sweating body and remounted his horse. The mutant ghetto seemed like a nightmare world, shifting in and out of reality almost at random, blurring into dream and then focusing sharply on hideous actuality. Without looking back, he spurred his animal and rode hastily out of the valley.

Somehow, the long week passed, and somehow Kesley endured it. Each day brought him closer to the audience with Winslow, when he would be called upon to act as assassin.

And he still had not a shred of plan.

Kesley's imagination had throbbed in constant feverish play all week, picturing and re-picturing the scene. Winslow — what did he look like? Suave and bearded, with dark tired eyes like Miguel's? Thin, pallid? Bloated?

It didn't matter. There was *a* Winslow on the throne, faceless and personalityless, and surrounding him were blurred shadows of courtiers: a priest perhaps, a few generals in formal armor, men like that. Kesley saw himself kneeling in the Duke's long hall, rising to advance on nerveless legs to the throne —

Plunging a knife into the Ducal bosom.

Firing an echoing pistol shot as he rose from obeisance.

Leaping forward and throttling Winslow on the throne.

Actually, he knew, it would not be that way. A Duke had an eternity to lose at an assassin's hands, and would be expected to surround himself with protection. No one, not even Miguel, would place himself at the mercy of anyone begging audience simply for the sake of "amusement." There were too many years to be lost.

Yet Kesley's active mind continued to develop a multitude of alternative methods for the killing, and always the picture ended with the moment of death. He found himself unable to project the action past the actual assassination; the sequel escaped his mind completely.

Seven days passed and, on the eighth, Kesley and Duke Winslow were to come face to face.

On the morning of the final day, Kesley rose early. Sleep had been intermittent during the just-ended night, and he left his quarters wearily shortly after dawn. On foot, he wandered through the awakening city, in full regalia.

By now it was generally known that ambassadors from Miguel's court had been in Chicago for the past week, and he drew uneasy stares from the curious early risers. He walked on, down one cobbled street after another, smelling the early morning smells of fresh air and the fresh food offered in the stalls.

The bright sunlight was glinting off Winslow's palace, sending down showers of scattered light. *Winslow is awakening now*, Kesley thought. *For his last morning. After four centuries he's come to his final day.*

Suddenly hungry, Kesley turned into a food shop that appeared a few feet away.

"Good morning," the proprietor said unctuously.

Kesley swung himself down into a booth without replying. After a moment, he looked up. "Coffee," he said.

"Certainly, *señor.*"

The white-uniformed counterman seemed delighted to be serving one of the South Americans. He bustled out officiously from behind the counter and put the cup before Kesley.

He tasted the coffee. The synthetic beverage was tepid, slightly oily. Nevertheless, he forced himself to finish it, then sat broodingly in the booth staring at the gray film of dinginess that overlay the empty cup.

"Something else maybe, *señor*?"

"No — nothing," Kesley said. "I'm not very hungry."

"Too bad, *señor*. Has the trip north disturbed your appetite? The food you're accustomed to —"

*Damned chatterbox,* Kesley thought, irritated.

"My appetite is fine." He dropped a coin ringingly on

the counter and walked out, into the warm, stale morning air.

Glancing around tensely, he let his hand slip to the hilt of his dagger. He caressed it absently for a moment, scowling. The minutes were crawling by like snails; the audience with Winslow would *never* come.

Dispiritedly, he turned his steps back toward the hotel. The desk-clerk looked idly as he entered.

"*Señor?*"

"What is it?" Kesley snapped.

"The man from Duke Miguel — have you seen him?"

"What man?" Kesley asked, puzzled.

"He arrived while you were out — a small man with a heavy mustache. His horse was nearly dead; he must have come in a great hurry."

Kesley frowned. He was expecting no one from Miguel. Hope flashed brightly: perhaps it was a last-minute reprieve for Winslow, and thus for Kesley. Perhaps, he, thought, it was a cancellation of the assassination order!

"Where is he?" Kesley asked hurriedly.

The desk-clerk jerked his head upward. "He went upstairs. Oh, about ten minutes ago. I guess he's still there."

"*Gracias,*" Kesley said. With sudden excitement he dashed up the stairs, threw open the door, and looked around.

No one was in the outer room of the suite. From within came no sound — not even the usual boisterous horseplay of his men. Cautiously, Kesley opened the inner door. Within, he saw Santana huddling over his breviary in his usual chair.

"Santana?"

There was no reply.

"Padre?"

The priest appeared to be totally absorbed in his reading. Annoyed, Kesley crossed the room and grabbed Santana roughly by the shoulder. The plump Archbishop spun limply, sagging backward as Kesley touched him, and dropped heavily from the chair.

Kesley paled. The red velvet of the Archbishop's robes was stained with a deeper red, already turning a crumbling brown. A knife had been thrust through the folds of fat that covered the priest's heart, and had found its mark. Santana had attained the martyrdom he coveted.

"Feliz! Domingo!" Kesley shouted. His voice sounded harsh, dry. "Luis! Where are you?"

He strode to the adjoining door and threw it open — and his men, as if they had been held back by a spillway, came pouring forth.

All six rushed out and, Kesley saw, there was a seventh with them, a small dark man who was apparently the courier from Miguel's court. Kesley leaped back and had his pistol and knife out almost before his mind was aware that he was under attack.

The gun barked. One man fell. The courier leaped forward, knife-blade high; Kesley sidestepped and ripped through the flesh of the man's back with a fierce downstroke. Turning quickly, he kicked a third man in the stomach, and backed toward the door.

They had no guns, but they outnumbered him six to one. Tossing his mantle to one side for greater freedom, Kesley chopped downward with the knife and drew blood again, while one of the grooms sidled toward him and slit his arm shallowly with a rapid lick of his blade. Kesley fired again, and the man fell.

Then he managed to bull out the door and down the stairs, with the five remaining South Americans thundering after him. At the first landing he paused to fire; a body tumbled toward him, and he caught the small man and wedged him crossways in the stairwell just as the other four approached. Kesley ducked as a thrown knife whizzed past his ear, and kept running.

He dashed out past the astounded clerk and into the courtyard. The hotel's ostler, a tall, bony old man with walrus mustaches, was puttering around Kesley's horse, rubbing it down with the tenderness a skilled groom would devote to a choice animal.

"Get out of the way, you idiot!" Kesley yelled as he entered the court.

Bewildered, the old man looked up, smiling mildly.

"Your horse is not yet curried, sir, and —"

"Out of the *way*!"

Kesley shoved the oldster to one side just as the four swarthy assassins swept into the courtyard and swarmed toward him. The old man tottered and took a couple of staggering steps that led him straight into the path of the South Americans; Kesley, mounting his horse, winced sympathetically as they collided with him and threw him roughly to the ground.

But the delay allowed Kesley to mount his animal and, even without spurs, he was able to bring the horse under quick control. He wheeled it toward the onrushing assassins. The magnificent beast whinnied and plunged forward.

Surprised, the South Americans yielded before this frontal attack; one aimed a knife blow at the horse's flank, but Kesley's boot caught the man's face and sent him reeling away. Kesley charged through the South Americans and out of the courtyard into the main thoroughfare.

He rode three or four blocks, then pulled up, gasping for breath, and guided the horse into a side-street for the moment. For the first time in the last six minutes, he had a chance to evaluate the situation:

Point: Santana was dead.

Point: his six men had turned against him, and only their stupidity and his agility had kept Kesley from sharing the Archbishop's fate.

Point: someone had arrived from Miguel's court shortly before.

Therefore, Miguel had changed his mind and had ordered the assassinations of Santana and Kesley. Or *had* Miguel changed his mind?

Perhaps this entire expedition had been a complicated way of wiping out a troublesome Archbishop?

Kesley's fingers quivered. Anything was possible — *anything* — when dealing with immortals.

*"Betrayal and betrayal again,"* the mutant Lomark Dawnspear had prophesied. And the mutant had been right.

For one reason or another — or perhaps none at all, Kesley thought coldly — Miguel had betrayed him.

And the counter-betrayal? Kesley smiled. Fifteen minutes ago, he had been steeling himself for the work of assassinating Duke Winslow. Now he would, rather, swear allegiance to him. The decision was made quickly, for Kesley saw it was the only path open to him.

He rode out of the shadows and onto the main stem again, moving cautiously as if expecting to see the four small Argentinians charging madly out of nowhere toward him. But they were not to be seen; the street was crowded with Chicagoans going about their morning business, and a sickly aura of heat was starting to descend as the August day edged toward noon.

Clamping together his tattered sleeve over his flesh-wound, Kesley rode out and toward a mounted policeman who sat stiff and proud in his green-and-gold uniform, looking down on the pedestrians.

"Officer?"

"Yes, *señor*?"

The title pleased Kesley; that meant he had been recognized. "There's been a disturbance down at my inn. My men were drinking, apparently. They've assassinated His Holiness, and attempted to kill me when I returned from my morning walk."

"How many are there?"

"I killed three in escaping. There are four left still at large down there."

The policeman drew a whistle and uttered a brief, subsonic blast. Almost instantly, a second mounted man rode up, and at his request Kesley repeated the story word for word.

"I'll go down there," the first officer said.

Kesley turned to the other. "Would you conduct me to the Palace? I feel I should seek sanctuary with the Duke until affairs are more stable."

"Of course."

Together they rode down the winding road that led to Winslow's Palace. The policeman was a man of few words; once, he asked if Kesley had any idea why he had been attacked. Kesley shrugged without replying.

For the first time, Winslow's rosy palace seemed to Kesley a place of refuge rather than the place where he undoubtedly would meet his death. He smiled grimly. Assassins had become assassins' victims; the wheels had turned, and the positions on the board had altered. For Santana, it had been check and mate; Kesley had escaped, through no fault of Miguel's.

But what if Miguel's messenger had come too late? Suppose Kesley had already seen and killed Winslow?

Kesley frowned; it was impossible to divine just what Miguel's real motive was. But now there would be no more dealings with Don Miguel.

A phantom thought struck him, and his lips curled upward. What if Winslow were to engage him in similar service and send him back to assassinate *Miguel?*

It was possible. Anything was possible, Kesley thought dismally. Anything was possible at all, in this chess game with all moves masked.

They drew near the palace. As usual, the guard at the gate inquired what business Kesley had within.

"I have an audience with the Duke," Kesley told him. With great punctiliousness, the gateman disappeared into his tower and returned clutching a lengthy appointment sheet.

"The audience is at two," Kesley said impatiently, as the gateman's eyes wandered all over the sheet.

"Indeed so," the guard replied after a moment. "And I believe it's no more than ten now. Duke Winslow will see you in four hours, no sooner, *señor.*"

Kesley wiped away sweat and fought down an impulse to cut the guardsman down with an impatient blow of his dagger. "It's an emergency. Tell the Duke that. Tell him that the Archbishop's been assassinated, and that I must see the Duke now!"

A flicker of interest crossed the guard's eyes. "I'll tell him that. Wait here."

Ten minutes later the guard returned. "Go in," he said laconically.

"You need me any more?" asked the policeman at Kesley's side.

"No — thanks, you've been very helpful." He handed the man a coin; and as an afterthought, he gave one to the gatekeeper as well, and entered.

A *déjà vu* emotion filtered through him at the sight of the interior of Winslow's Palace grounds. There was the same broad courtyard as at Miguel's, the same distant entrance. This time, though, a cold-faced man in Imperial uniform was waiting for him.

"I'm here to see the Duke," Kesley said.

The guard nodded. "Certainly. Duke Winslow will see you at once, s*eñor*. Please follow me."

Kesley followed. The great inner doors swung open, revealing a brightly-lit throne room on the ground floor. A row of unblinking retainers with halberds lined the room; there must have been twenty-five on each side, Kesley thought.

His throat parched at the thought of the task he would have faced trying to escape from this room after assassinating Winslow.

On a raised dais at the far end, beneath an immense figured shield and between two dark columns of glossy, grained onyx, sat a man who could only have been Duke Winslow. For the first time in his life, Kesley approached the man who ruled all of North America — the man whose life he had, not so long ago, pledged to take.

# SEVEN

WINSLOW had none of Miguel's crisp, compact muscularity, Kesley saw, as be hesitantly approached the throne. North America's Duke sprawled as massively across his gleaming white metal throne as the broad continent he ruled did across its hemisphere; he was an enormous, ponderous, obese man. Winslow's sobbing intake of breath was plainly audible even at the distance Kesley maintained.

"Your Highness," he said, and knelt.

"Rise," Winslow ordered. His voice, like Miguel's, was deep, but Winslow's voice had a soft, throaty liquidity to it that was most unlike Miguel's compelling boom.

Kesley rose and faced Winslow squarely. The Duke's features were blurred and indistinct, misshapen by the billowing puffs of fat that sagged from his cheeks. He wore a thin fringe of golden-red beard which screened a thick, many-chinned throat.

"Our audience was scheduled for this afternoon," Kesley said, since Winslow was evidently waiting for him to speak. "However, a change of schedule was made necessary by —"

"I have heard," the Duke murmured lazily. "News

travels swiftly here, sir. The Archbishop lies dead in an inn, is that it?"

"Dead at the hand of his own servants, Duke Winslow. Betrayed."

"Indeed?" The sleepy eyes of the gross-bodied Duke stirred; Kesley observed that behind the outward facade of sloth lay the nervous reflexes of a cat-keen intellect. "Betrayed? And by whom, *señor*?"

Kesley glanced uneasily around the room. "May we be alone, Duke Winslow?"

Chuckling the Duke said:"Certainly not. My life is much too important to me, young one. But you can speak freely here; the word of my court is sacred."

"Very well, then. I'll begin at the beginning." Drawing a deep breath, he said, "I was sent here to assassinate you."

Around Winslow, courtiers paled and reached for their weapons at Kelsey's flat admission, but Winslow himself showed no reaction whatever. It was infuriating to see the slow smile finally spread over his face. "How unfriendly," he observed at last.

"I had no intentions of actually carrying it out, of course."

"Of course." With biting sarcasm.

"I accepted the order in an attempt to free myself of Don Miguel's power. I had every intention of swearing allegiance to you, and —"

It seemed to Kesley that some ugly thought had passed at that moment through Winslow's mind and, disconcerted, he halted. Then, recovering, he continued:

"On the other hand, Archbishop Santana came here with the definite intent of doing away with you." However, this morning a courier arrived from Miguel, instructing our retinue to set upon us and kill us."

"A noteworthy aim," Winslow said. "One which, I take it, was only partially accomplished. Why are you telling me all this?"

"I want to expose Miguel's treachery. I want to make everything clear to you, show you what's been going on." Kesley spoke with desperate sincerity now.

Winslow laughed suddenly, his entire body quivering. "This is very funny," he said, when he had subsided. "Miguel sending men here to assassinate me — and then having his own assassins assassinated!" He narrowed his eyes and peered curiously at Kesley. "Why do you suppose he would do a thing like that?" he asked.

Kesley moistened cracking lips. "It is not for me to understand the ways of Dukes, Sire."

"I hardly expect it of you."

"Then —"

"You wish to enter my service?" Winslow asked. "It is strange that a former assassin would beg me to gather him to my capacious bosom. It is an amusing idea."

Suddenly Kesley felt like an insect being toyed with before having its wings plucked. Dizzily he glanced at the long rows of halberdiers standing like carven images, at the wax-faced courtiers grouped about Winslow's throne, and for a bewildering instant he thought that this was all some kind of dream from which he would soon wake and find himself back behind the plough, awaiting Tina's call to lunch.

"I never intended to strike a blow against you, Sire," Kesley lied humbly. "You believe that, don't you?"

"Of course I do," Winslow said gently, and without any trace of sarcasm. "Perhaps that's why Don Miguel decided to blot you out. However," he said, sighing, "I'm afraid you represent as great a threat to the Twelve Empires as has ever been born, my young friend."

He gestured to a hawk-faced man in somber robes standing to his left.

"Lovelette, take this man and convey him to the dungeons. Tomorrow, he's to be executed. Is that clear?"

"Certainly, Sire."

It had happened so quickly that Kesley did not fully understand it. One moment he had been on dangerously thin ice but managing to keep aloft; the next, he had plunged through into utter cold.

He felt thin fingers bite into his bicep, and a low voice say, "Come with me."

Two halberdiers advanced mechanically and took their posts at either side of him. Numb, he allowed himself to be marched away from Winslow's presence, with an infinite series of maddening *whys* screaming at him all down the long hall.

Why this sudden reversal on Winslow's part? Why the execution order? This, not Kesley's switch of allegiance, was obviously the *"betrayal again"* Lomark Dawnspear had foretold.

As Kesley was led from the Ducal presence, he heard Winslow's sardonic chuckling coming from behind. Tomorrow, he thought bleakly, it would be the headsman who would chuckle.

He had changed his coat once too often. Going to Winslow had proved a fatal move.

Kesley resolved that if he ever escaped from Winslow he would stay as far as he could from all the Dukes. Life was hard enough without making one's self subject to the caprices of life-jaded Immortals.

But, as the dark corridor leading to the dungeon opened out before him, he saw clearly that there was little chance of an escape this time.

During the rest of the day and the long night that followed, Kesley, alone in the darkness, had plenty of time to think.

He was in complete isolation, somewhere in the depths of Winslow's palace.

He had been thrust in; microrelays had clicked, and a heavy metal door had whirred creakingly closed. Air came filtering in from a dimly-visible grid in the ceiling, twelve feet above. There was no furniture in the cell, not even a cot. He could stand, or he could lie.

He stood for a while, pacing the length and breadth of the cell until that palled, and then he stretched out full length to wait for morning. There was no point wasting energy in fruitless escape tries; he had determined very quickly that his cell was proof to any attempts.

One dull gray thought flickered monotonously through his consciousness: tomorrow his life would end. That wasn't so bad, he thought; everyone dies — everyone but the Twelve. What hurt more was the rasping realization that he had never really lived at all.

What had he done, in the twenty-four years he'd had? Twenty of them were blank, cloaked by darkness more complete than the inkiness that surrounded him in the cell. He had lived and farmed in Kansas, he told people, but he knew it was false, and van Alen, whoever *he* had been, had known it was false.

Van Alen had confronted him with the naked lie he had been living, and it had hurt. Probing the past caused pain. All right. Blot out twenty years, begin life four years ago, ignore the mystery that cried to be solved.

*What kind of world is this,* he asked himself, w*here you never start to live?*

He had never known the rules. He never knew who made the moves, who played the game. Unseeingly, he had shunted from one pattern of action to another, without ever understanding the world he was in. It was ironic. A world carefully tailored for simplicity, a world scrupulously designed by its proprietors to avoid the complexity that had destroyed the previous civilization — and here he, after twenty-four years, was going to his death uncomprehendingly.

Something was terribly wrong with a world like that,

Kesley thought. Perhaps its goals had been good, once. But as the Immortals had moved timelessly on through the years, they had grown remote from the charts and maps of society, and begun to play some inscrutable, unfathomable game of their own.

"It isn't fair!" he said out loud. His protesting voice echoed weirdly in the confines of the cell, bounced back grotesquely from the metal walls. He knew that if there were a light in the cell he would be able to see his own distorted image on their shining surfaces. It would be a mocking clown-face, laughing at him for his own ignorance.

But there was no light. There was only darkness, and the silence of solitude.

And then, after hours passed, there came the faint humming sound of relays clicking in the massive door.

*Morning already?* Kesley wondered.

Time had passed; he knew that. But so much time? Was so little left?

The door was undeniably swinging open.

He had remained alone for almost a day and a night, and had returned no answers to his many questions. Shrugging, he waited for the Duke's men to take him away. *Maybe there aren't any answers,* he thought dismally.

He heard soft padding footsteps in his cell, and felt a cool hand grasp his.

"Stand up," a whispered voice said.

Wondering, Kesley pushed himself up from the floor.

"You're not the headsman," he said.

"No. The headsman waits for morning."

"Isn't it morning yet?"

"The hour is four," the strangely familiar voice whispered. "The Palace lies asleep."

Dimly, Kesley realized that this was some sort of impossible rescue — unless, that is, it was another hoax. Frowning into the impenetrable darkness, he said: "Who are you?"

There was no answer. But gradually a faint glow enveloped the cell, flickered warmly for a bare instant and died away.

"Dawnspear!"

"Speak quietly, friend. It was not easy persuading the guards to sleep."

Kesley rubbed his eyes, tried to peer into the darkness. The momentary slow of light had revealed the bizarre, piebald mutant towering above him.

Cautiously, Kesley extended his hand and felt the rough, cool skin of the mutant's bare chest as if to confirm his vision.

"What are you doing here, Dawnspear?"

"There are those who would not have you die," the mutant replied. "Winslow and Miguel know you. Two Dukes are in league to take your life, now. They can be dangerous enemies. Come."

Dawnspear grasped Kesley's hand firmly and guided him forward. As they passed through the open door of the cell, the metal began to swing shut again.

Kesley heard a faint clang as the cell closed.

Outside, in the dim light of the dungeons, Kesley made out sleeping forms lying here and there, slumped over their weapons. Guards.

"Did you drug them?" he asked.

"They were very sleepy," Dawnspear said ambiguously. "We must hurry, now."

They glided through the dungeon together, the man and the mutant. Kesley walked on tiptoe, moving delicately as if he were walking on the fragile surface of a dream; at any moment he expected Dawnspear to vanish and the entire illusion to drift into nothingness.

But then he smelled fresh air instead of dungeon mustiness, and he knew he was free.

"The gate is open down there," Dawnspear said, pointing. "The guards are lost in slumber."

Together they crossed the palace grounds and passed through the gate. Kesley turned to the gaunt figure of the mutant to demand some explanation, but Dawnspear had released his hand and was pointing toward the distance.

"Within a minute they will all be awake. You will be missed. Flee now, while you have the chance."

"Wait a second! How did — why — ?"

Kesley's whispers died away impotently. Dawnspear had slipped away silently into the night. *"Dawnspear!"* he called harshly. There was no reply.

*There never are answers when you call,* Kesley thought sourly. He wheeled, looked back at the sleeping

Palace. Lights were beginning to flicker on here and there; the mutant's influence had ended, and the sleepers were waking.

He was free to fly. Once again, he was his own master, bound to no one.

The guards stirred within the walls. He could imagine their dismay when they found him gone. Wrapping his cloak tightly around him, he edged off into the night.

A horse, first. Then, out the walls some way or other, and to freedom.

Both Winslow and Miguel would be hunting him, why, he could not say. But both his fealties stood revoked; his Dukes sought his life.

Well enough, Kesley thought. He had no debts to either Miguel or Winslow.

Once again he stood alone. Where to, now?

He thought of Narella, in Buenos Aires. She would be waiting for him to come back — or was she, too, only part of Miguel's scheming. He didn't want to believe that.

Van Alen had told him he belonged in Antarctica. Suddenly the image of the mysterious continent rose in his mind. He saw a vast wall. Nothing more was visible.

It took only a moment to frame a resolution. Find Daveen. Find Narella.

*And then,* he thought, *to Antarctica. To Antarctica!*

# EIGHT

THE SLEEP-WRAPPED city was dark and silent. Kesley raced down the quiet streets, cutting laterally once to avoid the yellow glare of a wandering patrolman's swinging sodium lamp.

He knew he had to move quickly. The city's gates would, of course, be barred, and he had no desire to try the lakefront way of leaving Chicago. He was no swimmer, and the lake, unguarded though it was, seemed endless. There was only one way out.

Pulling his richly-brocaded cloak around him, he looked ahead for some sign of the night patrolman who had just passed. Finally he found him, far down the opposite street, swinging his lamp as he made his routine rounds.

Cautiously, Kesley began to advance.

The watchman's broad back was turned; a heavy truncheon hung at his side, and the butt of a pistol gleamed in a holster. His lamp cast long shadows down the empty street.

Kesley sidled up behind him and clubbed downward efficiently with the side of his hand just as the watchman noticed the advancing shadow behind him. The man had half-turned when Kesley's hand cracked sharply into the column of his neck below his left ear and jawbone, and the watchman emitted a feeble gagging cry and fell. Kesley caught him neatly, grabbing the all-important lamp.

Moving quickly and smoothly, he stripped the patrolman, donned his clothes, and bound the unconscious man with his ambassadorial robes. The guard stirred; Kesley stunned him with the blow of the truncheon and dragged him into the courtyard of a small, private dwelling. Stuffing him into a garbage bin that stood outside the door, he straightened his clothing and stepped back to the street, swinging the lantern nonchalantly.

Moments later, horses' hooves thundered down from the Palace, breaking the quiet. Acting the part of a good watchman, Kesley ran out into the darkened street, holding his lamp up so its brightness would blur his face.

"What's going on? Where are you coming from?"

Two or three riders passed, ignoring him.

"I say, stop!"

A fourth rider leaned down from his horse. "Duke's guard, watchman. We're chasing an assassin!"

"Assassin? The Duke dead?"

"Heaven forbid. No; it's one of those South Americans. The Duke ordered him executed, but he escaped!"

"Dreadful," Kesley exclaimed, and released the bridle. The horse sped away into the night as another wave of riders followed down. Winslow, aroused, was probably sending his whole guard corps out to search for the fugitive.

Lights were going on all over the city now. Sudden bright, yellow eyes winked down from unshuttered windows. Kesley stepped back into the shadows and let five more horsemen go by.

A sixth came down the road. Kesley flagged him down with his lantern.

"What's going on, friend?"

"Haven't you heard? We're chasing an escaped assassin."

"What's that?" Kesley assumed an expression of horror. "What did he look like?"

"Big man in royal robes. One of those South Americans."

"No! I just saw one go into that house over there." He indicated a home which had not yet awakened to the clamor of the streets. "I'm sure it was the South American," Kesley continued. "I was going to ask him where he was going, but then I saw he was an ambassador and —"

There was no need to chatter further. The horseman, his mind set on medals, was dismounting.

"Which house?" he asked tensely. "That one?"

Kesley nodded. "Want me to help you?"

"That's all right," the guard said. "Stay out here and tend my horse. I'll go in and look around."

"Good luck," Kesley said. He let the man take six steps toward the silent house, then whipped out his truncheon and brought it down with skull-crumpling force. Hastily he dragged the man behind a low, bunchy shrub, ran back to the street, and clambered aboard the waiting horse.

As the animal began to move, yet another wave of guards swept down from the Palace. Kesley fell in with them, peering grimly forward into the night as they rode. They dashed in, clattering up the main street and splitting off there to explore any byway where the fugitive might be hidden. Atop his horse — a scale-covered, dusky mutant with many-jointed legs — Kesley choked off a chuckle and forced his face into the solemn mask of the dedicated pursuer.

In the morning, the elaborate, half-mythical tracking devices would be brought into play: the needle-snouted, mechanized bloodhounds of legendary dread, the whirling radar parabolas, the ingenious screens and devices inherited from a culture long dead. It wasn't much of a secret that the Dukes maintained many of the taboo devices of the Old World, and used them for their private ends. Miguel's closed-circuit TV, Kesley thought, was an example.

But the bloodhounds wouldn't be called out till later. Right now the reaction was one of simple hysteria; heads would be rolling at the Palace if Kesley were not found at once. And, he thought, riding atop a Ducal horse, clad in Ducal uniform, it wasn't too likely that they were going to find him.

He glanced ahead. The guards were riding together, forming an anxious little circle. Evidently someone had called a halt and was about to organize a systematic search.

Further ahead, the towers set in the wall ringing the city were lit; the guards there had been roused as well, it seemed. Kesley surreptitiously cantered out of line and cut off down a dark side-alley, taking care that none of the guards were following him.

A few minutes later he reached the West Gate — smaller than the other three, and lightly guarded. Drawing his horse up before the guard-tower, he shouted:"Open the gate, you idiots! The assassin's escaped, and he's heading west."

"What are you saying?"

"I said *open the gate*. I'm Duke's guard. You're holding things up. The assassin's out there at large someplace!"

The door swung back.

"Thanks," Kesley yelled. He kicked the mutant's scaly hide to make the beast spurt ahead. He raced through the open gate and out of Chicago. The confused shouts of the guards echoed faintly in the distance as he urged the horse on.

Breaking out into the flat country that ran westward, he rode hard without any direction or destination in mind. Once he looked around and saw three riders about two and a half miles back, pelting steadily after him.

They were on to him then. He hadn't fooled them completely. But it had worked well enough to get him clear of the city and, if he could put more space between himself and Chicago before they turned the hounds on him, he'd be all right.

The road veered suddenly and split into a network of forks. Almost without thinking, he grabbed the south fork and urged the horse on. He didn't know the country at all down there, but there were cities — Peoria, St. Louis, Springfield, Cairo way down on the river. Somewhere between those empty names, he had heard there was a Mutie City — a regular refuge for mutants, a walled city of some sort where not even Duke Winslow's hand could reach.

He bent low over his horse's stringy mane and urged the gasping beast on.

Glancing back, he saw his pursuers — and dim in the night was something dull and metallic grinding toward him down the flat road.

Bloodhound.

They had the hounds out after him already. Winslow wasn't going to let him escape lightly.

Shortly after sunup, his exhausted horse stumbled and fell, pitching him to the ground. Kesley rolled to his feet, glanced once at the animal's splintered leg doubled beneath its body, and looked back. No sign of his pursuers now.

He destroyed the horse with a single bullet and started moving, on foot, through the underbrush. He had no idea where he might be, except that he was somewhere south of Chicago.

Through the rest of the morning he hacked his way through the wild vegetation that had sprung up in this uncultivated area. Exhausted finally, he stopped near noon to rinse some of the sweat from his face at a clear blue brook.

Wearily, he scuttled away from the brook and started to get to his feet, without success. He remained kneeling, staring at the quivering tips of his fingers, smelling the warm morning air and listening to the singing of the untroubled birds, and finally slumped forward, face down in the fertile soil, and slept. He had been awake almost fifty hours.

Later, Kesley felt gentle hands slide under his body and scoop him up. Foggily, he opened one eye and fought to focus it. Deep in his mind, he was struggling toward wakefulness, acutely aware he should flee but unable to make his exhausted body respond.

"Let go of me," he murmured, clawing fitfully at the hands that held him.

He blinked. "Where are the hounds? Don't let the hounds near me."

"There are no hounds," a purring voice told him. "Winslow's men turned back hours ago."

Some of the cobwebs cleared from his brain. "No hounds? You're not from Winslow?"

"Look at me and see."

The hands released him and slowly Kesley turned. Standing behind him, arms extended uneasily in case Kesley should topple, was a graceful, seal-like creature with glistening, golden-brown skin. A slit-like mouth was bent into a clumsy smile; narrow eyes gazed warmly at him.

"I'm . . . very tired," Kesley said.

The mutant nodded gently. "You should be," he said. He took a step forward, and caught the exhausted Kesley just as he began to fall.

# NINE

SANCTUARY — for a while.

"So I'm not to be allowed any rest," Kesley said bitterly. "Three days here and you're tossing me out, is that it?"

He glared sourly at the little group of mutants facing him. "Well?"

"You've been here three days," Spahl pointed out. The seal-like mutant shrugged sadly. "That's three days longer than any non-mutant's ever spent in this city, Kesley. We can't keep you here much longer."

"Why do you want to stay here?" asked Foursmith, an angular, knobby-looking mutant with a row of inch-long red nubbins protruding through the flesh of his back. "You've got to get going, you know. Daveen's not here."

"I don't know *where* Daveen is!" Kesley said. "Can't you let me catch my breath?"

"You'll have to leave tomorrow," Spahl said. "We'll give you a horse."

"Thanks."

This was the third day since Spahl had rescued him in the forest and brought him to Mutie City; they had fed him and rested him, but now they insisted that he leave.

He couldn't blame them; the city was a refuge for harried mutants, not a harbor for escaped turncoats. They ran the risk of incurring Winslow's displeasure by giving him sanctuary. Yet, he thought, as long as they'd admitted him they might as well have let him stay long enough to get his bearings, to have some of the furor over him die down.

Well, at least they'd taken him in. A small blessing, but a real one.

"I'm sorry," he said humbly, walking to the window of the room they had given him. He looked out over the variegated city below — strange and motley compared with the neat regularity of all Empire-built cities.

"I'm imposing myself, and I'm acting like a fool." He wet his lips. "I'll go whenever you want me to."

"Don't misunderstand," Foursmith warned. The mutant with the extended vertebrae was the current head of the mutie enclave. "We're not throwing you out. We think you should leave, that's all. For your good and ours."

"Agreed," Kesley said. In the street below, a two-headed woman was making slow progress pushing a perambulator in which squirmed a many-armed monster-baby. He shuddered. He still was not used to such sights.

This was the world's genetic refuse heap, the city where the alien race in mankind's midst could live in peace and security. Gradually, Mutie City was enfolding in itself the mutants of the Ducal cities; here, the grim souvenirs of the time-shadowed great war could walk unmolested.

He could see the logic behind the agreement of the Dukes granting Mutie City total independence. The mutants came here and, gradually, the contamination of their genes would be localized, the cancer of mutation penned into one tiny area. Kesley wondered whether, on the day when the last mutant had left the Twelve Empires and entered Mutie City, the Dukes would bomb the city to shreds and thus restore mankind's genetic homogeneity. It was a terrible thought.

He turned. There they were, Spahl and Foursmith and Ricketts and Huygens and Devree, each one looking as if he had come down from a different world. They ruled the city.

"Why did you take me in?" he asked.

"There were reasons," Huygens, the double-header, said resonantly.

*Always reasons*, Kesley thought. *And everyone knows them but me.*

"This Daveen — he's not a mutant, is he?" Kesley asked.

"No," Foursmith said. "I saw him once, in the court of Duke Winslow. He is very tall, without hair, and blind. He's not one of us."

"And you don't know where I could find him?"

"You might try the Colony," Foursmith suggested. "He might be in hiding there, among the other artists. At any event, the Colony is safe from Winslow, too. Perhaps you could stay there for a while."

"Good enough," Kesley said.

The Colony sprang from the blue-green grass of Kentucky like a sprawling, segmented worm. Its architecture bore no resemblance to that of any city Kesley had ever seen; broad, rambling, almost ramshackle, it presented, an even more disorderly appearance than had Mutie City.

He wheeled the exhausted six-legged horse the mutants had given him up the final stretches of the roadway, looking around cautiously as he rode. It had been a tense but, happily, uneventful tourney down from Illinois.

The Colony, like all other cities, was walled. But it was as if a different architect had planned each segment of the wall. Here, it was high and carved from blocks of pink granite; there, it was a lazy stile of limestone. Towers of black basalt capped the wall at irregular intervals.

He rode toward the gate — an open gate. Pulling his mount to a halt as he approached, he turned toward the guard.

"Who are you?" questioned the guard, looking up from a notebook. Kesley saw a series of interlocking doodles scrawled on the man's page.

"My name is Kesley. I'm here seeking sanctuary from Duke Winslow. I'm also looking for a blind poet named Daveen. Is he here?"

"He has been," the guard answered. "You armed?"

"Pistol and truncheon," Kesley said.

"Leave 'em out here. You can pick them up when you're leaving."

Kesley didn't like the idea of parting with his weapons, but he seemed to have little choice. Reluctantly, he surrendered them and rode inside, into what seemed to be a park.

A fantastic array of houses was visible beyond the park. For a moment, Kesley thought he had wandered into a lunatic's asylum. Then he remembered it was simply an artists' refuge.

A nude girl stood unashamedly in the center of a lawn not far away, and clustered about her, sketching furiously, was a group of painters. Beneath a live-oak behind her, a fat, balding man squatted on the ground, playing a wooden flute. Elsewhere, other members of the colony seemed to be busying themselves at their various interests.

Kesley tethered his horse at a hitching-post just inside the main wall, and looked around for someone who might be in authority.

After a moment, a girl in a brief halter and shorts approached him. "Hello, friend. My name is Lisa. Where from?"

Her voice was clear and firm. Somewhat hesitantly, Kesley said, "Chicago, mostly."

"Oh? What do you do?"

"I don't understand," Kesley said.

"Paint, sing, write? Light-sculpture? Architecture? Come on," she said impatiently.

"I see. No, I'm not an artist. I'm . . . just here visiting. Looking for someone."

"That's nice. Who?"

"A poet. Daveen the Singer, they call him. Is he here?"

The girl frowned. "Daveen? I recall the name — but I don't think he is living here now. You'll have to ask Colin about that. He remembers everything."

"Where can I find this Colin?" Kesley asked.

"Over there." She pointed to the group surrounding the lechers busy sketching Marla. "He doesn't any more about sketching than I do, but he loves to look at a pretty body. He's the bald one, right down in front. You'd better not bother him now."

"I''ll wait," Kesley said. He could hold his own among assassins, but he could see that he was going sadly out of his depth here in the Colony.

The Colony was even more grotesque and wonderful a place than Kesley had imagined, in that first dazzling introduction in the park. After the darkness of the world of the different darkness of Mutie City, the Colony stood forth as a kind of beacon.

Total anarchy prevailed, for one thing. People lived where they liked, ate as they pleased, worked or did not work. There was always enough food. The Colony was self sufficient, insular, smug in its seclusion. And inscribed in deep-cut letters over the inside of the main gate were four words:

# DO WHAT THOU WILT

"The guiding motto of the Abbey of Theleme," Lisa explained, when Kesley commented.

"Theleme?"

"A reference to Rabelais," she said. "Oh, I see you don't know that, either. It's a book — I mean, he was a writer. You don't read much, do you?"

"No," Kesley said distantly, staring at the huge letters in the stone. *Do What Thou Wilt.* They were shattering words; he wondered what Duke Winslow's reaction would be if he ever had an opportunity to see them.

But there wasn't much chance of that. The Colony was even older than the Twelve Empires, having been established back in the days of the chaos by a group of artists and poets determined to preserve their way of life while the rest of the world crumbled about them. They had succeeded; and now, the outside world did without them. They had no part in Empire doings, and the Empire kept its distance from them. It was, Kesley, was told, all part of the uneasy balance in which the world was held. No one dared tip the scales.

He was welcomed to the Colony warmly, even though he was quick to make clear that he himself was no artist and that he was here solely in quest of Daveen. The night of his arrival they held an immense party, supposedly in his honor.

He recognized a few faces. The girl named Lisa had

appointed herself his guardian; she stayed close by his side. Somewhere else in the huge roomful of milling people, he spotted the man named Colin, looking like an aging Silenus with his baggy eyes and fuzzy crown of graying hair. He was engaged in animated conversation with the girl Marla, who had modeled nude that afternoon. Now, she wore a transparent plastic blouse and tights; it was an even more startling costume.

Finally, Kesley got to speak to Colin.

The balding man was very fat and very drunk, he noticed. He stared curiously at Kesley for a few minutes, then said, "You're the newcomer, aren't you? The one we're all here to honor?"

"I'm looking for a man named Daveen. You know him?"

"No," Colin said loudly. "Never heard of him. Want a drink?"

Kesley shook his head. He flicked a glance warily at Lisa, who was smiling enigmatically. "He's a poet," Kesley said. "A blind man. Lisa thinks she remembers him."

"Lisa will say anything. I don't remember any Daveen."

"Daveen? Who's talking about Daveen?" a deep voice asked. Kesley glanced to his left and saw a tall, burly, blond man with long curling hair. The big youth was smiling sweetly.

"I am," Kesley said. "I'm looking for him."

From somewhere in the background came the discordant shrill of a strange musical instrument. Kesley winced.

"What do you want Daveen for?" the blond boy asked. "You from the court?"

"I'm *running* from the court. Winslow wants to kill me. I have to find Daveen."

The tall youngster chuckled raucously. "Daveen hasn't been here in years. You'll *never* find him!"

An atonal blast of the weird music blended oddly with the harsh laughter that suddenly surrounded him. Defeated, confused, Kesley looked at the alien faces of the men and women in the room. It was as if they wore masks of desperate gaiety, hiding a deep inward brooding.

He realized it had been a mistake to come here. In the middle of the room, a lithe girl of about nineteen was taking off her clothes to the accompaniment of an ecstatic chant from a ring of onlookers; a spindly man of about forty was intoning what was probably poetry, and the blond boy had gone into a frenzied solo dance.

Distortion upon distortion, darkness within darkness. Kesley felt cold and alone. At his side, Lisa clung tightly to him, sliding her hands playfully over the flat, hard muscles of his chest, giggling and whispering. The party was reaching a peak of wild license now.

This was what happened when walls closed around people, he thought. The mutants in their city; the poets in theirs. The Dukes in their Empires. And somewhere, far to the frozen south, the Antarcticans behind their blockade. They all interlocked, meshed in a tightly-geared procession to nowhere. Grimly, Kesley watched the blond boy dance himself into exhaustion, watched the girl in the middle of the room whip off her one remaining garment and stand totally naked. Lisa was chanting, *"This is the way the world ends, this is the way the world ends."* It was probably a line from some poem. But it was more than poetry, thought Kesley. It was truth.

Truth.

# TEN

WHEN MORNING finally came, Kesley had long since decided to leave the Colony.

As the first rays of dawn broke, he rose and made his way over the huddling sleepers in the room. Lisa stirred; the poetess had slumped over yawningly more than an hour before. On the floor, between the sleepers, lay remnants of artistic achievement — strewn manuscripts, curious statuettes, musical scores, musical instruments and such things. Kesley carefully avoided stepping on them. He wanted no contact here.

"Where are you going?" Lisa asked, looking up. Her eyes were red and raw looking; the copper mesh of her blouse was stained with the thick amber fluid of the drink she had laughingly poured between her breasts at some wild moment of the night before.

"Outside," Kesley said.

"Wait a minute. I'll go with you."

Shrugging, he stepped outside and she followed him. The dawn was coming up fresh and clear, with dew hanging brightly in the air. It would, Kesley thought, wash away the pollution in the air from last night's party. He tightened his lips nervously.

"Which way is the gate?" he asked.

"That way. Are you leaving? Why? Don't you like it here?" Impulsively, she tugged on his arm. "Answer me, Dale."

He looked wearily down at her. "I don't like it here. This place is poisoned. I want to get away, before I catch whatever all of you have."

"I don't understand you."

"Naturally not. Look, Lisa, you and your fellow esthetes have been bottled up in here since — since — when? The year two thousand?"

"John Harchman came here to found his colony in 2059," she said as if repeating a catechism.

"The year doesn't matter. You've been cooped up five hundred years. And what do you have to show for it? Great works of art? No — just drunken parties."

"We've produced wonderful things. Colin's done a glorious visomural, and the sensotapes —"

"You've produced nothing," Kesley said inexorably. "You create for yourselves — each other, at best. But not for the world outside."

"The world outside doesn't want us."

"Wrong. We don't understand you. And it's as much your fault as ours." Kesley turned away. "Leave me alone, Lisa. I should never have come here. I want to leave."

The jagged, violet blades of knifegrass glinted strangely in the morning sun. Kesley waited patiently while his hungry horse grazed. Mutant horse, mutant grass, the cycle held firm. Spindly, six-legged animal nibbling sharp-toothed, man-high grass. The purple blades blended with the blue-green of the Old Kind.

There had been no bombs over Kentucky, but the wind had carried the drifting seeds, brought the zygotes of the strange new grass down here to this unruined land. Now, a tough network of roots dug into the turf, and from them sprang the metal-sharp grass the atoms had made.

Kesley rode south, his mind full of melancholy thoughts.

The trail had completely trickled out — if there had been a trail. He was chasing phantoms, will-of-the-wisps.

Daveen, for instance. Who was he? A blind courtier who had vanished some four years previously, whose name van Alen had happened to drop and link with Kesley's. What relation did Daveen have to him? He didn't know. What relation did van Alen have, for that that matter.

But he was searching for Daveen. The search had led to the Colony, but that was a dead end. Daveen had been there, and Daveen was no longer there, and that was all anyone could or would tell him.

Then, Narella. A hauntingly lovely girl — but so, for that matter, was the poetess Lisa. Narella was somewhere in Buenos Aires, at Miguel's court. Would he ever see her again? Again, he didn't know.

The horse plodded onward toward the mysterious

city of Wiener. Kesley knew nothing about the city that lay ahead except that Lisa had recommended that he go there. It was another island on the continent, untouched by Winslow.

The picture of Winslow came to his mind, and immediately after, that of Miguel. They were different and similar, the two Immortals: one fat and gross, the other lean and hard, both complex and unfathomable, both deep-eyed with the loneliness of the timeless man. Miguel had welcomed him to his service, sent him off on a deadly errand, then reversed himself and ordered his death. And Winslow had refused him sanctuary and condemned him to death as well. Doubtless there was now a price on his head throughout all of North and South America.

That left Antarctica, a complete unknown. Vaguely he recalled that that had been his original destination when leaving Iowa, months before. But Antarctica was about as accessible as the moon, Kesley thought.

Then he thought of the mutants: Lomark Dawnspear, the blind one who had unaccountably rescued him from Winslow's dungeon, and Spahl and Huygens and Foursmith and the others of Mutie City, far to the north. What of them?

Lisa. The Colony, shallow and desperate and decadent, rotten from within and unable to see it.

Tiredly, Kesley rode on.

Above, the sky was warm and bright, and the rolling hills of southern Kentucky were broad, beautiful, dotted heavily with the purple grass and the strange golden-leaved trees the wars had brought. The vegetation was the only hint here that there once had been devastation in the world; today, in this place at this time, it seemed as if everything had been perfect forever. But he knew that it hadn't.

He rode on. Wiener lay ahead.

A week later, the city of Wiener rose before him from the wide flatlands of Northern Texas. He paused, reined in his horse, looked at the low sprawling wall of metal that rambled out over the desert.

He urged the tired mutie on. Hooves kicked up dry bursts of yellow sand.

As he drew near he could see that the wall was solid from side to side. This was no encircled city; it was one huge building, probably sunk deep into the earth.

Sunlight glinted flashingly off the metal wall. Kesley squinted, saw a dot of brightness detach itself from the city and come humming across the sands toward him. The City of Wiener was taking no chances, apparently; they were going to intercept him before he got too close.

He waited for the vehicle to approach. As it drew near; he saw that it was unmanned, merely a hollow shell made of some bright metal, teardrop-shaped and empty.

"Please get inside," a dead-sounding voice requested. "We will take you to the city."

Shrugging, Kesley rode forward; the teardrop split

into halves. He guided his mount inside; the great door dropped closed again, and a moment later he was heading at a terrifying speed toward the metal city.

# ELEVEN

THE HUMMING teardrop sped across the empty wastes; within, through a clear plastic window, Kesley watched the metal building loom larger.

Then they were almost next to it, and abruptly a section of the building's gleaming wall opened. The teardrop shot in without reducing speed, slid along a banked incline that swung it in a wide curve through a vast enclosed area and gradually brought it to a halt. The teardrop split open again and, somewhat shaken, Kesley and his mount left it.

He looked around. The place was brightly lit despite the total absence of windows; the ceiling was some fifty feet above his head, and he could see stairwells spiraling down deep into the earth. Along one wall rose a shining mass of dials and meters, switches and complex instruments which seemed to be moving rapidly from one position to another sheerly of their own accord.

All around him were machines. He felt a strange queasiness. Machines were things to fear; they had destroyed the world, once. The sight of them, clicking and humming and carrying out their unknown functions, disturbed him immensely.

Hesitantly, he began to walk.

A long corridor sprang into being not far from where he stood, winding narrowly away and downward. He decided to follow it. But after he had proceeded no more than twenty yards into it, he discovered a brightly-lit, little glass cubicle set into the wall, a small room with a chair, a clock on one wall, and a coppery-looking grid set into the other. He decided to investigate. Tethering his horse to a bracket along the corridor wall, he pushed open the cubicle door, entered, and placed himself in the chair.

Instantly a voice said:"Welcome to Wiener. May we have your name for benefit of our memory banks?"

Alarmed, Kesley glanced around. The voice had seemed to come from the wall-grid. "Dale Kesley," he stammered.

"Welcome to Wiener, Dale Kesley." The voice was unemotional, dead-sounding. Kesley frowned.

"What sort of city is this?" he asked.

There was silence for a long moment; he heard strange cracklings and rumblings coming from the grid. Then:

"The City of Wiener was officially founded on August 16, 2058, by Darby Chisholm, C. Edward Gronke, H. D. Feldstein, David M. Kammer, and Arthur Lloyd Canby, professors of cybernetics at Columbia University, Harvard University, Massachusetts Institute of Technology, Colby Institute and Swarthmore College. The avowed aim of the five founders was to create a completely self-sufficient, automated cybernetic community in a relatively nonstrategic area of the United States, where experiments in non-limited automational control could be put into practice.

"The building of the City of Wiener was implemented by a government grant of three billion dollars and private contributions. Four sites were chosen: Juntura, Oregon; Lodge Grass, Montana; Wanblee, South Dakota; Wilder, Texas. It was the original plan of the founders to utilize all four sites and build identical cities at each, but the precipitation of war in 2059 made it unwise to divert energies to so large a project at that time, and the decision was made to limit the experiment to the Texas site alone. This later proved to have been wise, in view of the unexpected attacks on the three rejected sites in the apparently mistaken impression that they had been the ones chosen.

"The City of Wiener was completed on April 11, 2061, and the switch feeding the first input was thrown by Dr. Chisholm of Columbia. A series of cybernetic governors powered by a fusion-breeder reactor then took full control of operations, and the City of Wiener was officially born. It has —"

"All right," Kesley interrupted suddenly, realizing he was about to receive a detailed history of the City's activities over the past four centuries. "I'd like to see whoever's in charge here. The Mayor, or whatever."

"Question has no cognitive referent," the dry voice said. "'*Seeing*' the controlling body is out of the question, as no human is to be permitted access to the cybernetic governors under terms of the original City contract established, between the City of Wiener and its five founders in —"

Dumbstruck, Kesley said:"You mean a *machine* runs this City?"

"The question is inaccurate. The City is a machine. There are no human inhabitants."

Suddenly chilled, Kesley looked up at the grid at which he had been directing his words, and realized he had been holding conversation with a mechanical brain, not some remote City official. Moistening his lips, he said:"What does the City *do*?"

"Question is unclear."

*The precision of the mechanical mind,* he thought in amused irritation. He rephrased the question. "What functions does the City carry out, aside from the normal routine of — of self-repair?"

"The City maintains a record of happenings in the Outer World; this record is not completely available for examination at the moment, due to unsettled conditions without. The City supplies manufactured goods to those who request them, as prescribed by its founders. The City endeavors to supply information within the bounds of self-safety, likewise as prescribed. The City —"

"Does the City know of a poet named Daveen?" Kesley broke in.

"Question will have to be referred to Answering Banks."

A pause, then, in a somewhat altered voice: "Information incomplete on poet Daveen, no other name recorded, member of court Duke Winslow Chicago North America 2504-2521, left court 2521, current whereabouts unknown. Is full biography requested?"

"No." Kesley crossed his legs and stared broodingly at his boots for a moment. The entire City a vast sentient machine, then! No wonder the Dukes left it alone; they knew they would never have the strength to destroy Wiener, and so they preferred that the machine-hating populace never learned of the City's existence.

He found himself greatly curious about the City. His imagination was engaged by the implications of a city-sized mechanical mind; he who had never dealt with any machine more complex than a pistol, who had had only fleeting acquaintance with the remnants of the Old Days, was fascinated by this mightiest machine of all.

"What can you tell me about Dale Kesley?" he asked on a sudden impulse.

Again silence — silence while photon-tracers raced over cryotronic circuits searching for information. Then: "Dale Kesley, farmer, entered Iowa Province June 21, 2521, no previous record, left Iowa Province undetermined time in spring of this year. Entered City of Wiener unaccompanied except by one mutant horse Type VX-1342 on October 8 of this year. Further information is lacking."

"Thanks," Kesley said hoarsely. His first twenty years were blank to the City, too. "Mind if I look around the place a little?"

"Limited examination of City of Wiener is permitted,"

the metal voice said. "Your animal has been removed for care and will be returned to you upon request."

He glanced through the thick glass window of the cubicle and saw that it was indeed so. While he had talked, unseen hands — *hands?* — had taken the horse away. Led it to pasture, Kesley wondered?

He wandered through the silent halls of the complex city, observing with a sort of quiet horror the chill efficiency with which the robot mind carried out its daily routine.

The City *was* populated. Kesley came across the inhabitants immediately after leaving the glass-walled cubicle. They were man-sized robots of blue metal, rolling on noiseless treads, equipped with opposable-thumbed hands and filament-ended tentacles and wiry grippers, seeing out of bright electrophotic eyes and gazing evenly ahead with expressionless, shiny faces.

One of them was squatting over an immense heap of coiled tape which was growing almost as fast as he could scoop it up and feed it into the chittering maw of some glossy data-eater in one wall.

Another was repairing a mass of tangled circuits in an exposed ganglion behind a section of wall.

Still another of the mechanical men stood at some distance away, holding a segmented tube to the mouth of Kesley's horse. The horse had its jointed scaly lips pressed tight against the tube, and was eating or drinking with evident contentment.

Air-conditioners hummed gently in the background, keeping the atmosphere pure and dustless. From the floor came the throbbing of some mighty engines far below. Kesley wondered just how deep in the ground the City penetrated.

All around, computers chattered and whistled. Kesley felt his astonishment growing with each moment. And beneath the astonishment, there was a mounting resentment at the Ducal philosophy that had blanked such achievements as this from the world.

*Machines have destroyed civilization*, people said. But had they? No; not the machines. It was man's *use* of the machines; the machines themselves were impartial, as disinterested in the currents of human affairs as the moon and the stars.

Yet the Dukes had risen to power on a program of throttled technological development. Fleetingly, the thought went through Kesley's mind that the Dukes had made a mistake. If only —

He stopped, feeling a shiver of pain. Once again he had touched some reverberating rawness in the deep layers of his mind; once again, a forbidden thought.

In sudden inspiration he turned toward a grid set in the wall near him.

"Can I get information from you?" he asked.

"Answering circuits are functioning."

"Can you tell me anything about Antarctica? Anything at all?"

Silence for a moment. "Do you mean Antarctica

before or after removal of the ice?" the voice asked.

"Afterward — I guess."

"We have no information on Antarctica after 2062,"
the machine said. "Ice removal was completed in 2021,
and settlement proceeded along with rapid technological development. In 2062 Antarctica ceased all contact
with the rest of the world."

2062 was the year of the Great Blast, Kesley thought.
And Antarctica had drawn the curtain.

He shrugged and walked away, taking a seat on a
curved metal stanchion projecting from the floor. Somewhere, locked in the obstinate memory banks of this
computer-city, might be the information he needed to
orient himself in the world, the missing data that everyone maddeningly withheld from him. But where to find
it? How to get it?

Suddenly the City's voice said:"Dale Kesley!"

"I'm here. What do you want?"

"You will have to leave at once. We will tolerate a
delay of no more than five minutes, plus or minus one."

"How come? Why can't I stay?"

"The City of Wiener faces armed attack if you remain here. Therefore, you must leave."

*Very logical*, Kesley thought coldly. "Armed attack
from whom?"

A section of the wall near him rolled away, revealing a
mammoth screen that showed the outside desert with startling clarity. Kesley saw figures huddled along the horizon, marching forward. An army. Duke Winslow's army.

"They're from the Duke, aren't they?"

"Yes. They've come to get you."

"And you're just going to turn me over to them?" Kesley asked horror-stricken.

"We are simply are requesting that you leave. We do not wish to risk an armed attack upon yourself."

"You can defend yourself, can't you?"

"We are not afraid of the Duke. We simply wish to avoid any conflict as unnecessary expenditure of materiel and effort. You now have three minutes, plus or minus one, in which to leave freely."

Sweat began to pour down Kesley's back. He glanced at the screen, saw Winslow's advancing forces. They had somehow tracked him to Wiener.

But the City *couldn't* throw him out now! It just wasn't fair!

Grimly, he started to run.

He charged forward toward the long shadowed corridor and heard his footsteps ringing loudly as he ran. The corridor was a helix that wound deeper and deeper into the Earth. Kesley ran, feeling the pure cold air whipping fast.

Gleaming blue mechanical men turned to look at him as he went by.

"Two minutes, plus or minus one," the machine warned. Its voice seemed to be everywhere. Kesley saw the familiar grids studding the wall at regular intervals.

He had to hide. He had to avoid the City's commands, avoid Winslow, stay here where he was safe. He found a dark alcove and stepped in. There was a door; he opened it, stepped through, and found himself in the midst of an intricate network of machinery, row on row of relay and stud.

"One minute, plus or minus one," the ubiquitous voice said. Kesley scowled. There wouldn't be any escape, it seemed. He kept running.

"We have requested that you leave. Your time is now exhausted, and we must remove you."

Kesley whirled desperately and saw four of the metal men coming toward him. They seized him gently, grasping him in the thick paws of their upper arms. His fists thudded against the solid metal of their chest, bruising his knuckles but failing to stop their advance.

They lifted him and began to move, sliding forward at an incredible pace up the long corridor and toward the beckoning iris of an opening door.

# TWELVE

ONCE AGAIN, he was fleeing.

*Always on the run*, he thought bitterly, as the mutant horse flashed over the prairie, its six legs pistoning as it drew away from Winslow's men.

The City had been considerate; the City had been kind. The teardrop-vehicle had not desposited him sprawling at Winslow's feet, and for that mercy Kesley had to be grateful.

The four implacable robots had carried him effortlessly toward the opening door; the uncomplaining horse had already been led through the opening and into the waiting vehicle. Still yelling, Kesley had been crammed into the silvery vehicle, and it had started away from the confines of the City.

Winslow's men were advancing steadily. The City had ejected Kesley to save its own titanium skin, its own guts of transistors and cryotrons.

He was ejected from the vehicle and left in the midst of the hot sands, with Winslow's men still a distant green-and-gold blur on the horizon. For a moment Kesley had stood there uncertainly, staring back at the City that had cast him forth; then, mounting his wobbly-legged horse, he began to ride.

He headed north, back the way he came. Winslow had obviously pursued him through Illinois, perhaps tracked him from Mutie City to the Colony to Wiener — but the City had avoided disaster by ejecting him.

Now, northward.

Returning to the Colony was out of the question for many reasons. Returning to Iowa would probably be fatal — Loren and Lester, good subjects, of the Duke, would turn the fugitive in without giving the matter a minute's thought. South America was as dangerous a place as Winslow's lands, and the Empires beyond the sea were impossible to reach. There was little traffic between the Americas and either Asia, Europe, Africa, or Australasia, and none whatsoever with Antarctica.

If he allowed Winslow to catch up with him, it would mean sure death. But one solution presented itself. *I'll return to Mutie City,* he thought, spurring the bony beast on. *That's one place where Winslow won't dare to come in after me.*

Kesley squirmed in the saddle and peered around. Men were breaking off from the column of horsemen and were starting to follow him.

He gave the reins another tug. Whatever it was the City had fed the animal, it was propelling the beast like gasoline. The mutant was covering ground in a rocket-like fashion. But Kesley knew the pace could never last.

And, sure enough, the mutie began to falter after another half mile, to drop back and lose ground. Four of Winslow's men were still on the trail; Kesley computed that he was somewhere near the Oklahoma border, and hoped no border guards would trouble him as he passed into the adjoining province.

He had a knife and a truncheon; the pursuers probably had pistols. He wouldn't last long once they caught him. They'd gun him down on the spot.

And he'd never know why.

The horse gave out shortly after high noon. Kesley managed to guide the winded beast into a thicket off the main road, and dismounted there, crouching in hiding while the mutie gasped for breath and shook its sweating sides.

Before long the four pursuers arrived on the scene. For an instant Kesley thought they would simply keep riding past, but he heard voices commenting that the trail of hoofprints ended up here. He tensed, knowing they would soon be searching the bushes for him.

"You go that way," someone said.

Kesley tethered his tired horse and backed away a little deeper into the underbrush. Several minutes passed.

Then a figure in the green-and-gold Ducal uniform appeared, a tall, dark-complected man with bare, burly arms. He clutched a drawn pistol in one hand.

"Hey, here's his horse —" he started to say, and Kesley leaped. His attack was the sudden, quick strike and withdrawal of the forest serpent; he sprang from the bushes, clubbed downward with the truncheon, withdrew again as the man fell. He waited a minute; then, seeing none of the other three approaching, Kesley quietly stole out and seized the fallen man's pistol. Now he was armed.

Cupping his hand over his mouth to muffle his voice, he shouted, "I got him in here!" Then he ducked back behind a thick-boled tree.

"We're coming, Gar!"

Three more uniformed figures stepped into the clearing. Kesley squeezed the trigger three times and they fell, their faces frozen in utter astonishment. Kesley felt suddenly unclean; he had murdered three men, injured a fourth. And those three did not know why *they* had died, either.

He freed his own horse and slapped the weary mutant on the flank. "Go ahead, fella. You're free. You've done your job." He could take his pick from the four Ducal thoroughbreds waiting on the highway.

Sadly he stepped over the fallen bodies. The man he had clubbed was still breathing; he lay in a sticky pool of his blood. Kesley knelt, saw the ugly, raw wound on the man's skull, the welling blood matting the dark hair. Wedged in the soldier's sash was a grimy, folded piece of thick paper. Kesley drew it forth.

It was on the Ducal stationary, with the familiar heraldic watermark that he had seen on so many tax vouchers in his farming days. The inscription, in large, dark, slightly smudged type, was a simple one:

# WANTED

### For High Treason
### Against His Highness,
### Duke Winslow of North America

> Dale Kesley, farmer, of Iowa Province, also known under the false name of Ramon, Ambassador from Duke Miguel of South America.
>
> The said Kesley, having entered His Highness' court on pretext of an embassy from the Court of Bueos Aires, did make an attempt on our Duke's life. Kesley is sought urgently. A reward of fifty thousand dollars is offered for his corpse.
>
> The said Kesley is six-feet-two in height, with closely-trimmed blond hair, full lips, nose set somewhat unevenly on his face. He will probably be wearing stolen clothing and riding a stolen horse.

That was all. Kesley whistled; fifty thousand dollars was a staggering sum of cash to offer. And they wanted his *corpse*; Winslow had no interest in anything but a dead Kesley, then.

He would have to look sharp. With fifty thousand riding on his head, every loyal subject from Texas to Maine Province would be ready to sell him to the Duke.

He lived a hazardous existence on the way north, eating off the forest and staying out of the way of anyone official-looking. He travelled mostly by night, creeping along cautiously during the day and making up the delay by galloping furiously once the sun had set.

Generally he had no difficulties. Crossing from Arkansas into Missouri nearly caused trouble, when he blundered into a border patrol searching for someone else. He never found out who it was they really wanted; two of the guards stopped him, stared at his face in the light of a flickering match, and, after a tense moment or two, incredibly sent him along his way.

In central Missouri he wandered into a hobo camp. Four bedraggled-looking men were squatting around an iron pot in which bubbled some sort of stew. Kesley had not eaten all day; he rode up to them and dismounted, keeping a hand hovering near his weapons in case they should recognize him.

They didn't.

"Come join us, brother," one of them invited. He was a heavy man with a bulbous red nose.

"Thanks. Don't mind if I do." Kesley lowered himself into the circle round the fire.

"You from hereabouts?" a lean man of perhaps sixty asked grudgingly. "Don't spot your face."

"I'm an Illinoiser," Kesley said. "Spent some time down in Texas. Now I'm heading home again."

He helped himself to a potful of stew. The stuff was hot and bubbling — too hot, really, to taste, which perhaps was a sort of blessing, Kesley thought.

"Little squabble down near Arkansas, that's all. They were hunting someone or other, and took me for him."

"They do that, sometimes," the red-nosed man agreed. "Times are tough now. The woods are full of Winslow's men."

"Oh? Something up?"

"Seems someone tried to kill the old bird," the red-faced man said. "Guess he got fed up after all these years."

"I suspect it was the Duke from South America," the lean man said. "The Dukes are out for each other, mark my words!"

The fire flickered and sent a spiral of smoke curling into the trees. Staring at it, Kesley found the sight oddly soothing. He took another sip of the stew.

Chuckling, he said, "They must be chasing this guy all over the country. I'll bet there's a nifty price on his head."

"Seventy-five thousand, that's what it is!"

Kesley frowned. Had the reward increased so fast — or was this just the exaggeration of ignorance? It didn't much matter.

"I'd like to catch some of that money myself, you know. Seventy-five thousand, huh?"

The red-nosed man laughed raucously. "You know, if I was the guy, maybe I'd turn *myself* in, for that kind of dough!"

Maybe you would, Kesley thought, watching the ghostly shapes the fire took. Anybody would do anything these days.

"What would you do if I was the guy?" he asked suddenly.

"You?" The red-nosed man seemed to stiffen a little. "Why would *you* want to go killin' Dukes?"

"Yeah," Kesley said. "That's right, I guess."

He moved on later that night, leaving his companions behind. They seemed happy there in the forest. He toyed with the idea of telling them the truth before he left, but rejected the idea. There was no telling how they'd react to the confession — but seventy-five thousand was a lot of money, and he didn't want four more deaths to his score.

He kept riding. He passed through Missouri and up into Illinois, following the Mississippi up from Cairo. The year was well into late October and the evenings were chilly. He rode quickly; the horse he had captured was a smoothly-functioning, full-blooded traveling machine.

Up through Illinois, until finally the broad expanse of Mutie City was visible through the dawn haze. For the first time since being cast out of Wiener he had the feeling that he was approaching safety. Flight was over — for now.

Of course, the mutants had told him not to return. But this was an emergency; surely they'd let him in.

He entered the city shortly after morning. The mutants were stirring, going about their early-day business. It seemed a savage parody of a normal city's routine. The shops were crowded, and what difference did it make if shopkeepers' heads were of spongy blue flesh and shoppers had the arms of lizards?

He felt terribly weary. As he entered the city, he was not surprised to see Spahl coming toward him.

"Hello," he said, dismounting.

"We expected your return," the seal-like creature said without preamble of formality. "We knew when we asked you to leave that you would be back."

"I want to rest," Kesley said. "This time don't throw me out."

He allowed Spahl to lead him to the room he had occupied on his earlier visit. A group of mutants congregated; he recognized Foursmith and Huygen. There were some others, stranger and more bizarre than any he had yet seen.

It was odd, Kesley thought, that the one place on Earth he could go for sanctuary was to this repository of freaks. Angrily, be brushed the thought away. The mutants were — well, *people*.

"I've been to the Colony and to Wiener," he explained. "I couldn't stay there. Winslow's hunting me all over the country."

"We know these things," Spahl said quietly. "We have followed your path, Kesley."

"And — ?"

"We have decided the time has come for you to go home. You've been long awaited and we'll make sure you get there safely."

"Home?"

"Now your life is in danger. You endanger anyone you come in contact with. Obviously you must not remain in Winslow's territories any longer — or Miguel's."

"And therefore," Foursmith added when Spahl ceased, "we will send you forth. For your sake and ours."

Huygens, the man of two heads, said:"Besides, Daveen has been found."

"What? Where?"

"He is in Antarctican hands now. We sent him there but recently. He waits for you. Spahl, is it time?"

"Not just yet," said the seal-man. "Kesley, will you remember what we're doing — *later*? We're buying our lives from you. Will you remember that?"

"I don't understand a thing," Kesley said wearily. "I don't even think I want to understand. But yes, I'll remember. Sure." He rocked forward on his chair, dizzy, confused.

The mutants gave way, and a new one entered the room — a small, very pale man, normal except for the huge circumference of his skull.

"Edwin is a teleport," Spahl remarked casually.

"What —"

Suddenly Kesley, felt himself struck by a blinding bolt of force; it spun him around, whirled him as if he were in a maelstrom, lifted him up. He saw the smiling faces of Spahl and Foursmith, saw all the mutants dwindle behind him. He rose, higher and higher, spinning vertiginously, frozen in an instantaneous moment of time. Space hung beneath him.

Then he began to fall.

# THIRTEEN

FOR A moment, after the spinning stopped, Kesley imagined he was back on the sands outside Wiener. Then, gradually, his eyes began to shift into focus. He looked around.

He was in a room. That was the first thing to grasp.

His senses told him he was in a room, high, with bare walls that glowed of their own inner luminescence.

Good. He was in a room.

He was no longer in the *same* room that he had been in Mutie City. He was sure of that, too. The big-skulled mutant named Edwin had lifted him — *teleport,* Spahl said? — and had sent him somewhere.

He was somewhere else than Mutie City.

Patiently, his quivering mind reassembled the world of sense-constructs and data from which he had been hurled. He was not alone.

He made out the other figure clearly: a tall, old man, sitting upright in a webwork chair halfway across the room. The old man's eyes were closed; he grasped a spiral object, unfamiliar looking, in one hand. His skull was hairless.

Kesley assembled the data.

"The mutants finally found you," the other said. His

voice was deep and musical, a rich basso with an underlying harmonic tremolo. "They were searching quite diligently, you know."

"Yes, they found me," Kesley said. "I'm here. Where's *here*?"

"Antarctica," the old man said.

Nodding, Kesley absorbed the fact and added it to those he had already. The jolting shock of the teleportation was beginning to wear off now; having been plucked from the spatial framework, he was returning to it, somewhere else. His mind emerged from its numbness.

"You're Daveen the Singer," he said calmly.

"I am Daveen," the other admitted.

Kesley studied the old man, realizing with a shock that he had almost forgotten the contours of Narella's face until seeing the girl's features mirrored here on Daveen's untroubled face.

A tense silence prevailed in the room.

Finally Daveen said:"Five years has changed you, young friend. You've lost your youthful face; I see beginning wrinkles where smoothness once was."

Kesley frowned. "How do you know? You're blind, aren't you?"

"The blind have ways of seeing. Besides, it's not a difficult matter to guess that after what you have been through —

"Just what do you know about me?" Kesley interrupted. "Who are you, anyway?"

"I was," Daveen said softly, "for many years, poet

and singer to the Court of Duke Winslow. Five years ago I participated in the first of your many rescues — the first time Winslow attempted to have you killed." He chuckled musically. "Poor slovenly Winslow. Every time you fall in his clutches, some blind man comes along to lead you to safety."

"You rescued me? From what?"

"That I cannot tell you yet. The Duke warns me that I must be very careful with you, that I must not swamp your mind with too much information at once."

Kesley looked around at the bare, luminescent walls, at the smiling figure of the gaunt-faced, old, blind man sitting opposite him. "Which Duke?"

"The Antarctican Duke. The man who has searched so long and patiently to bring both of us together. You see?"

"Yes," Kesley said faintly. "*He* brought us here. But where were you?"

"I fled from Winslow, five years past, after doing what I did. I sought refuge in Scandinavia and sang for the Duke there until Winslow's men found me and forced me to fly. I returned to North America, lived for a while at the Colony — I believe your odyssey brought you there as well — and when life there became unbearable, I vanished."

"Where? How?"

"There are ways," Daveen said. "When one knows the arts of the mind, one can do many things. I went into hiding. It was the only way for me to remain alive.

Winslow sought me with desperate urgency, for I had betrayed him. Miguel had my daughter."

"I know."

"I continued to live in North America under Winslow's very nose. It was a good joke; now that I'm free, I must let Winslow know about it. He has a fine sense of the ironic."

"Where did you stay?" Kesley prodded.

"I lived in the ghetto."

"Among the *mutants*?"

"I *was* a mutant. You knew me as Lomark Dawnspear."

For a moment Kesley rocked crazily in his chair; things seemed to wheel in a dizzy arc around him.

"What?" he finally asked, recovering himself.

"Mental projection, complete; constant hypnosis."

"Dawnspear was blind, too," Kesley recalled suddenly.

"Yes. It pleased me to retain the image of the blind man who saw so well. Dawnspear was blind. Otherwise, he was a complete fabrication. I invented a false background for him, persuaded people that he had always lived in that house in that part of Chicago. And they believed it. Unable to do anything else, I lived camouflaged, not knowing how urgently I was sought."

"And then I came to Chicago."

"Then you came. And stumbled into Winslow's grasp exactly as you had done before. And once again reached the dungeons. Again, it was necessary for me to rescue you. I did it once before, as Daveen. Five years ago. You came to Winslow's court, and he delivered you to the headsman. I intervened."

"Why? How?"

"You loved my daughter. Furthermore, I thought you should not die."

"I loved her even then?" Kesley asked, astonished.

"Yes. She does not remember, nor do you but you loved each other. When Winslow ordered you killed, I determined to save you. I hypnotized your jailers, slipped into the dungeon, freed you, led you out. It was a gross violation of my oath to Winslow."

Daveen paused, and Kesley stared intently at him, waiting for him to go on. There was something grotesque about this calm, matter-of-fact relation of actions he had been involved in and yet remembered nothing about. Reality seemed to slide yawningly from moment to moment. He had loved Narella five years ago? He had been at Winslow's court, and been sentenced to death?

Possibly. But it was as if those things had happened to someone else.

"Go on," Kesley said hoarsely. "What was I doing at Winslow's court? For God's sake, Daveen, *who am I*?"

The singer shook his head slowly. "No. Not yet. Let me go on, and you'll learn the rest in proper time."

"Very well," Kesley said, mollified.

"I took you from the prison, as 'Dawnspear' did just recently. I attempted to contact those who would receive you safely, but could not. Failing this, I had to make provision for your safety. I therefore placed you in full hypnosis, wiped out all knowledge of your past background, and substituted a pseudo-biography in which you had been born in — Kansas Province, I believe. It was a slipshod job, but I was in a hurry. Were there inconsistencies?"

"Yes," Kesley said. "There were."

"I feared as much. But it was the best I could do, at the time. I took the precaution of webbing in a pain-threshold that would keep you from probing your own past too deeply. Then I had you transported to Iowa Province, safely out of Winslow's way, and established you as a farmer there. It was a secure, rhythmic life; tied to the soil, you would remain healthy and unmolested. Later, perhaps, I would be able to take you from the farm and restore your identity.

"I returned to Chicago. My daughter asked where you were; I found it necessary to block her memories of you to prevent unhappiness. They can be restored as well, when the time comes. Curiously, you and she came together again later, neither knowing who the other was — and the result of the meeting was the same as before." Daveen smiled. "This, I think, should amply prove the strength of your love, at any rate."

Kesley coughed. Nervously he said:"So you left me in Iowa. You never came to get me — or were you van Alen, too?"

"No. I was not van Alen. My plans were interrupted; Winslow discovered how you had been freed, and in anger ordered my execution. I fled; Narella was given to Miguel as plaything."

"He calls her his daughter," Kesley pointed out.

"Fortunately. Miguel is going through a paternal cycle; for the moment, he no longer feels fleshly desires. Narella was sent to be his mistress — but became his adopted daughter instead. Dukes are difficult to fathom in advance."

"I know that well."

"To continue: I fled. You remained in Iowa Province. Those who loved you sought you, finally found you."

"You mean van Alen? He tried to bring me here — to Antarctica."

"Yes. He failed; you and he were separated. Once again you drifted into dealings with the Dukes — and when they realized who you were, they immediately desired your death. Both Miguel and Winslow."

"*Why?* Why'd they turn on me like that?"

"For that," Daveen said, "the simplest answer involves the lifting of the first of the psychic blocks I laid upon you. Are you ready?"

"I've been waiting for this since you started talking."

Again Daveen chuckled melodiously. "In all your wanderings you've learned but little patience. Now you will begin to understand."

He held forth the object he had been holding. Kesley now saw that it was a musical instrument of some kind, fashioned of a dark-hued, glossy plastic. It had three hairfine strings running its length; at the top, above the bridge, were three white buttons.

"My music-maker," Daveen said. "My constant companion always. It holds the keys to your mind, my friend."

"What do you mean?"

"Listen."

Daveen touched the three buttons lightly with his long fingers, and a tone appeared, shimmering delicately, followed by a second and a third. They hung in the air, meshing their subharmonics, quivering and blending. It was, thought Kesley, like no music he had ever heard.

Daveen began to play — a slow, mournful, lingeringly lovely melody. Melodic lines intertwined in complex polyphony; Kesley found himself following the music with breathless excitement. It soothed and tensed him at the same time.

Daveen sang a deep, lulling, wordless chant. Beneath his voice the music swept to a gentle crest of subdued excitement, and Kesley felt his nerves quivering with expectation.

The music, strange, atonal now, shifting keys with impossible rapidity of modulation, held suddenly.

Daveen stopped.

There was complete silence.

In that silence, Daveen said, "One!"

And Kesley felt light flash numbingly through him.

He huddled in his chair while the frozen brain-cells at last discharged the information they had stored for nearly five years. The words went rumbling over his synapses, repeating themselves endlessly.

Finally it stopped. Hesitantly, he looked up at smiling Daveen.

Then he looked down at his hands — his own hands he had farmed with and killed with.

The hands of an Immortal.

"Me?"

It was almost impossible. But he knew it was true.

"You will never die," Daveen said.

"I will never die."

*"Two!"* said Daveen suddenly.

Kesley was thrown back in his seat by the unexpected, second data-release. When it was over, he looked up again, smiling.

"An Immortal and the son of an Immortal. Small wonder Miguel and Winslow wanted to kill me!"

The words of Winslow's sentence came drifting back now: *". . . you represent as great a threat to the Twelve Empires as has ever been born, my young friend."*

Of course! Twelve sterile Dukes, blessed with eternal life but cursed with the inability to reproduce — what would they do, how would they react when they knew that one line of Immortals, somewhere in Earth, bred true? That they were faced with the prospect of a gathering race of Immortals threatening their powers as the years rolled on?

"You see?" Daveen asked.

"I understand now," Kesley said. "They *had* to try to kill me. I was a menace — an Immortal who wasn't a

Duke, and whose children could breed true!"

He stared at his hands as if they were covered with suddenly alien flesh. "I wasn't a Duke, was I?" he asked cautiously. Anything was possible now.

"No," Daveen told him. "You were never a Duke."

Kesley smiled, thinking now of the centuries stretching endlessly ahead. "A king without a kingdom, then. Well, there's plenty of time for me to find one. But you still haven't told me who I am, Daveen."

# FOURTEEN

THERE WAS silence in the bare room for almost a minute. Idly, Daveen strummed his instrument; Kesley tensed, thinking another layer of his mind-block was to be stripped back, but Daveen was merely striking random notes.

"Well?" Kesley asked.

"The information you want is not mine to give."

"All right," Kesley said. He rose and stared down at the blind man. "I won't ask again."

He had asked too many people too many questions, without result. Now he would save his breath.

As he stood there, a door opened silently out of the wall.

"What's that for?" he demanded. Then, realizing the blind Daveen was unaware of the occurrence, he added:"A door just opened in the wall."

"Doors are for leaving rooms," Daveen observed.

"I'll take the hint." Kesley hesitantly stepped through — and saw Antarctica.

He was standing on a short, jutting balcony that hung a few feet out over the distant street below. Sudden vertigo gripped him as he looked down, down. It was five hundred — no, a thousand — feet to the ground!

Tiny dots of color moved rapidly far below on un-ceasing slide-ramps. Down the center of the street, graceful cars of blue and gold and red, topped with plastic bubbles, raced along. Buildings rose on each side of the street—towering edifices, mighty vaults of steel and plastic. Kesley sucked in his breath sharply.

The sky overhead was warm and bright, and just below the clouds, far in the distance, a curious, tingling, purplish light illuminated the sky. *That's the barrier,* Kesley realized. The intangible wall of force that sepa-rated Antarctica from the rest of the world.

It was a mind-numbing sight, this fantastic city. It was like no city he had ever seen in the Empires; it stretched to the horizon, tower after massive tower. A graceful network of airy flexibridges hung like gos-samer in the air, linking building to building far above street level.

And the city was shining.

That was the only way to describe it. The sleek sides of the huge buildings gleamed brightly in the warm daylight.

As Kesley looked out, it seemed to him as if so many thousand-foot mirrors blinked back at him.

He stepped back inside. Daveen had not moved.

"You've never seen Antarctica, have you?" Kesley asked.

The poet smiled. "I know what it must be like. How do you feel?"

Kesley thought of the shining towers and compared

them with the squat tenements of Chicago and Buenos Aires. "It's an incredible city."

"Yes," Daveen said.

With sudden bitterness Kesley said:"Why does the Antarctican Duke keep that barrier up? Why doesn't he invite the world down here to see what he has? Why must ninety percent of mankind live in squalor?"

"They want it that way," Daveen pointed out.

He fingered his instrument gently; a mocking note crept forth. Kesley remained silent in thought for a moment.

Then he nodded. "You're right. The Dukes see to it that nothing changes, that no progress is ever made. The Twelve Empires don't want any part of Antarctica, and Antarctica doesn't want any part of them."

Antarctica's Duke, for one reason or another, had raised an impregnable wall around his fantastic paradise. The Twelve Dukes of the war-blasted world had erected their own barriers. But who was to say those barriers could not be thrown down again? There was a *fourteenth* Immortal. And he was free to act.

Ten minutes ago such thoughts would have been nothing more than bravado. Now, Kesley knew, he held power in his hands.

"Daveen."

"Yes?"

"I'm going to leave. I'm going to go looking for the Duke. Is there anything else you want to tell me, before I go?"

A calm smile spread over the tired face. "Not now," Daveen said.

Another panel in the wall opened as if at Kesley's request, and without hesitating he stepped through. He found himself in a small rectangular enclosure whose luminescent walls were inlaid with tiles of a glowing green plastic.

"Down," he said, and the enclosure sank.

It glided downward with no illusion of descent, drifted through a thousand-foot shaft and came to a silent halt. A wall opened. Kesley saw that he was at ground level, in the vestibule of the great building.

He saw the people: tanned, happy-faced people who did not seem to notice him. They wore smooth, free-flowing tunics of what seemed like an uncreasable fabric; it put the finest robes of the courtiers of the Americas to shame.

As he paused in the vestibule, not quite knowing which way to turn, he heard a familiar humming sound, turned, and saw a mechanical man near him. It might have been a twin of the ones he had seen at Wiener.

"I give information," the robot said.

"How can I get to the Duke's palace?"

"Duke's residence is reached by travelling on slide-walk eleven blocks north to crosspoint, transferring to eastbound slidewall and continuing until destination. You will be aware when reaching Duke's residence."

"Thanks," Kesley said.

"Is any other information requested?"

"Not just yet," he said. He turned away and broke the photon beam that controlled the front door. It swung open. He stepped out onto the slidewalks.

There were five of them, he saw, running in a parallel series — five bright metal strips moving at different speeds. He was on the slowest of the five; it glided forward effortlessly, seemingly without friction. Carefully, he stepped to the adjoining strip, which was a little more crowded, and picked up speed. He became intrigued by the moving roadway and rapidly passed to the fastest of the slidewalks.

By that time, though; eight blocks had slipped past, and he hastily edged back to the slow walk. At the eleventh block, he cut off deftly onto the eastbound walk that intercepted the one he had been on.

Now he could see the Duke's Palace: a square, blocky edifice of lacy foamglass that was dwarfed by the towering buildings to either side. Remembering the awesome majesty of Winslow's and Miguel's palaces in comparison to the rest of Chicago and Buenos Aires, he thought it odd — and then not so odd — that Antarctica's Duke should affect a small, relatively unimpressive home.

The slidewalk brought him rapidly to shining door that fronted the Ducal palace. Kesley formulated his plan, set forth his demands in his mind.

It was a bold, rash idea. If it failed, he had lost nothing. And if it succeeded —

He stepped off the slidewalk. The Duke's Palace seemed to beckon.

Inside, a robot attendant came humming up to him. Kesley confronted the featureless face calmly.

"I'd like to see the Duke."

"Certainly. Have you an appointment?"

"No," Kesley said. "Tell him —"

"Just one moment," the robot interrupted. "I'll arrange for an appointment. Your name, please?"

"Dale Kesley."

There was the momentary clicking of data-sorters over memory banks.

Then the robot said:"Confirmation requested. Was the name Dale Kesley?"

"That's right."

"The Duke will see you at once, Dale Kesley. I will escort you to him."

A little surprised, Kesley nodded. "That'll be fine."

The robot glided away on its treads toward a lift-ramp; Kesley followed, suppressing his impatience.

He wondered if the Duke of Antarctica would be surrounded by long rows of halberdiers. Somehow he doubted it.

A pulse tickled annoyingly in the side of his throat as the elevator rose. The trip was brief; the door-panel was sliding open almost before it had closed.

The robot rolled out first and started off down a long, bright corridor. Kesley followed.

The corridor seemed to be endless. Finally, the robot paused before a richly-panelled door and touched a stud.

"Yes?" a deep voice said.

Inclining its speaking-grid toward a pickup embedded in the ornament of the door, the robot said:"Dale Kesley to see you?"

*"Kesley?"*

"Dale Kesley to see you," the robot repeated impassively. Kesley heard stirring within. He tensed; this was suspicious. Was it this easy to gain audience with a Duke?

He waited nervously for the door to open. He had been hired to kill Winslow; Miguel had begged him once to drive a knife into *his* breast. And now he was about to see a third Duke — the first he had any real motive for killing.

The door swung back. Another robot waited within.

"Don't tell me *you're* the Duke!" Kesley said, aghast. He had long since learned that anything was likely.

"Hardly," the new robot replied, with as much of an ironic inflection as a robot voice could muster. "The Duke waits for you within. Come."

Fingering the keen knife at his side, Kesley entered the Ducal chambers.

# FIFTEEN

THE ANTARCTICAN DUKE lived well, Kesley thought. His private apartments were sprawling, luxurious, with more than one strange echo of Miguel's room. For one, a wall of paintings looked down — but they were not oil works such as Miguel had, but paintings done in some curiously realistic technique that hardly seemed to involve brushwork at all. They were more frozen images of life than paintings, he thought.

In the distance he could see television screens, reminding him of the closed-circuit battery taking up one wall of Miguel's study. The robot led him on, gliding him from room to room.

"This is the Duke's room," the robot said finally. "You may go in."

Kesley approached the dark, paneled-wood door. It swung open without his touching it.

A man stood there, dressed in the customary Antarctican costume, smiling, his arms folded. Kesley's eyes flickered in surprise; then he crossed the threshold.

"Van Alen," he said.

The noble grinned. "Hello, Dale. I owe you an apology. I found it necessary to flee, back there in the woods. But I've been following your subsequent adventures with great interest, Dale."

"I'll bet you have," Kesley said. He studied van Alen's powerful frame, meeting eyebrows, wide-set eyes. "I never thought I'd see you again, but here I am. I suppose you're here to take me to the Duke. Well, I'm ready."

Van Alen's smile grew broader. He extracted a jewel-studded, gold case from his tunic, pressed a stud. A tiny yellow filament licked forth. He touched it casually to his wrist; a fugitive tingle of pleasure passed over his face.

"Electrostimulator," he explained. "Sensory heightening. One of my favorite vices; one that I had to leave behind when I made my abortive journey to Iowa Province."

"I'd like to see the Duke," Kesley repeated impatiently. Van Alen chuckled. "Look at my eyes, Dale." Kesley glanced up from the electrostimulator in van Alen's hand; his gaze traveled up over the glossy, green fabric of the noble's tunic, over his stiff reddish beard, his firm lips, the jutting nose, to the eyes.

The eyes.

The deep, tired, weary, all-seeing eyes of an Immortal.

Oddly, it came as no surprise. Double identity was almost the rule in the world, it seemed. Daveen and Dawnspear, van Alen and the Duke, Kesley and—who?

Kesley groped unsteadily toward a chair; it sprang forward and settled itself beneath him. "You, yourself—"

"Antarctica is mine, Dale. I went north to bring you here, but I failed. My life was threatened in the forest. I ran. An Immortal is jealous of his life. Remember the scream of fear when you first drew the knife on me, after I shot your wolf? That was *fright* — naked, crawling fright." The Antarctican shook his head bitterly. "I should never have left here."

"I've seen Daveen," Kesley said.

"I know. The otter sent him to me."

"Spahl?"

Van Alen nodded. "That's his name. You owe your life to him many times over, Dale."

"I owe my life to everyone at least six times, it seems," Kesley said sardonically. "It seems to be a game everyone likes to play — saving me."

"Spahl found who Lomark Dawnspear really was and sent him here. Spahl was the one who arranged to have you sent here, by the only method that can penetrate our Barrier. It was Spahl also, I believe, who discovered you in the forest when you escaped from Miguel."

Kesley frowned. "Enough of Spahl. I've seen Daveen. I know I'm Immortal, now."

"Of course."

"Why didn't you tell me?"

Van Alen spread his hands. "Would you have believed me?"

Kesley paused, thinking for a moment. "No," he said finally. "But when Daveen struck those notes on his instrument, I *knew*."

He rose and began to pace nervously. His booted feet sank deep into the glistening carpet that covered the entire room.

"I want to tell you why I came to see the Duke, van Alen. I mean that — I came to see the Duke as Duke, and the fact that he turned out to be you doesn't matter a damn to what I'm going to say."

Lazily van Alen touched the electrostimulator to his wrist again.

"Go ahead. I'm most interested."

"From what little I've seen of Antarctica, it's a wonderful place. It's the only place in the world where science didn't die with the Great Blast — except Wiener, maybe, and there aren't any people in Wiener. You've got technology, here; you've got a working society. I've only been here a few hours and I don't know *what* you have. But I do know this: you've got the power to knock Winslow and Miguel and the rest of them sprawling from their thrones, and break down the resistance to progress that the Twelve Dukes have so carefully built up."

The smile had left van Alen's face. The Duke was studying Kesley reflectively, his lips drawn into a tight scowl, his lean fingers knotted in the fringes of his beard.

Kesley moistened his lips. "For one reason or another, you've set up this impassable wall. You want to keep what you've got, and you don't want anything to do with the rest of the world to the north. Is this right?"

"This has been my policy," van Alen admitted.

Kesley glanced around uneasily. "Can you justify the policy?"

"I see no need to."

"All right," Kesley said. "Let me suggest an alternate policy: you step down from the throne and appoint me Duke. I'm an Immortal too, I've discovered lately; I'll take your job. And I'll break down all the barriers that keep the people of the world penned away from each other."

"Just how will you persuade me to allow this?" van Alen asked, with icy calmness.

*This is the moment,* Kesley thought. He stepped toward van Alen, seized the momentarily relaxed arm quickly, twisted it up behind the Immortal's back. At the same moment he drew his knife, touched it to van Alen's throat just below the beard.

"Miguel taught me that Immortals can be killed. He sent me off to kill one. I don't want to drive this knife home van Alen, but I will if I have to. Get your robots in here and dictate a message of abdication."

"If I don't —"

Kesley twitched the knife slightly. Van Alen winced.

"I can break your hold, you know," the Duke pointed out.

"Probably." Kesley remembered the time vn Alen had broken Kesley's grip in the Iowa farmhouse, had removed Kesley's hands from his throat as if he were a child. "But while you're doing that, I push the knife in. You don't have a chance. Will you dictate the abdication?"

"I've ruled here three hundred sixty years and more," van Alen said. "It's not easy to give up a throne in a moment after so long."

Again Kesley dug the knife in. This time, a few drops of blood trickled down, staining van Alen's broad collar. Immortal blood.

"Well?"

Sweat mingled with the blood droplets on van Alen's throat. "I agree to terms," he said hoarsely. "Snap on the recorder on my desk."

Kesley looked suspiciously at the knob mounted in the cabinet. "If this is a trick ——"

"No trick," van Alen said.

Kesley backed across the room without releasing his grip on van Alen, and spun the noble around. "Reach down and snap on the recorder yourself. I'll be ready with the knife if anything strange happens. Then start to talk."

Van Alen shifted the position of the stud with an extended finger. A faint hum resulted; otherwise, nothing happened. Kesley relaxed just a trifle.

"Talk," he ordered.

Van Alen said: "People of Antarctica, hear and believe this message.

"Today, in the three hundred sixty-second year of my rule, I am giving up my throne.

"I turn it over to the man named Dale Kesley — like myself an Immortal. He will rule you wisely and well, I am sure, and will lead you to greatnesses I never dared to attain."

"Thank you."

Van Alen shut the machine off. "There," he said. "When I touch the spiral lever, the message will be beamed on wide circuit to the entire continent. The robots will shift allegiance to you at once; the place will be yours."

"Touch the lever," Kesley said hoarsely.

Van Alen reached out — but as he nudged the control, a bright green beam licked out suddenly. Acting instinctively, Kesley jabbed at the Duke's throat with the knife.

There was no knife.

The knife had been whisked from his hand the instant the beam had shot forth.

Van Alen turned, easily extricating his imprisoned arm from Kesley's numbed grasp. His fist crashed into Kesley's stomach, rocking him backward.

*Cheated!* Kesley thought wildly. He recalled an earlier, forgotten resolution never to have dealings with Dukes again.

Mechanically he raised a fist to defend himself. Van Alen's attack drove through, and blows thudded against his face and chest. He tried to fight back; he hit van Alen glancingly on the shoulder, struck for his midsection. Another blow sent him staggering away.

Desperately Kesley leaped forward and flung himself on van Alen. They tumbled to the floor, rolled over several times, once with Kesley on top. Then van Alen began to get the upper hand. The Immortal was fantastically strong.

He rose to a sitting position atop Kesley, gripping both of Kesley's hands in one of his. He wiped flecks of perspiration from his chin and dabbed at the tiny cut on his throat.

"Sorry, Dale. In five hundred years I've learned a few tricks. That was a teleport beam; your knife's now somewhere in the main routing depot of my post office."

Kesley muttered a harsh, wordless curse. Then he said:"You'll kill me now, I suppose."

"For reacting the way I expected you would? Nonsense." Van Alen rolled off Kesley and stood up. Reaching to his desk, he pressed a buzzer and said, "Admit Daveen."

"Why do you want *him*?" Kesley asked.

"You'll see."

The panel glided open and Daveen stepped through, walking with uncanny assurance.

*"Three,"* van Alen said.

Daveen began to play the same haunting melody he had played before. Kesley, lying on the floor, waited uncertainly for the moment when —

"Three," Daveen said.

One crushing fact rolled down on Kesley like a shock wave. *One* fact.

He waited while its implications shuddered through him like subharmonics from Daveen's music-maker. His dazed mind evaluated the new datum.

"Of course," he said finally, standing up. "Why else would you have gone to Iowa Province looking for me?

Why else would you be so interested in my where-abouts?"

"You see now?" van Alen asked.

"I see part of it. I see that *yours* is the line of Immortals that breeds true, since I'm your son."

"I thought you would have guessed that when Daveen rolled back the very first layer of fog," van Alen said. "You didn't. But now you know *who* you are."

"And why — why —"

"Four," van Alen ordered.

*"Four!"* Daveen cried.

And Kesley began to understand.

# SIXTEEN

"YOU KNOW, now?" van Allen asked.

Kesley smiled wanly. "This isn't the first time we've had this discussion, then."

"No. The last time, though, you had no knife."

"If I had known who you were, I'd never —"

"Certainly," van Alen said. "You're not to be blamed."

"May I go?" Daveen interrupted suddenly.

Van Alen nodded. "Of course, Daveen. You've done splendidly."

"Thank you, sire," said the Singer gravely. Bowing, the blind man backed unerringly out into the adjoining elevator. Van Alen turned back to Kesley.

"You remember, now, the circumstances under which we last met in this room?"

"Yes," Kesley said. "I came to you — to ask you to abdicate in my favor, Father. You refused."

"And you ran away."

"What else could I do? You were Immortal; I was twenty-three, and you refused to leave the throne. I thought you were wrong in your ways."

"Twenty-three — and you wanted to rule," van Alen repeated reflectively. "Now, of course, you have the wisdom of mature years. Why, you must be nearly thirty, old man!"

"Twenty-eight. And I'm still aging. What was it Stohrbach said, your geneticist? That I'll continue to age until about the age of thirty and then stop?"

"Thirty-five. You haven't reached full maturity yet."

"But my cells show the regenerative pattern of an Immortal."

Kesley let the other newly-awakened memories filter through his mind.

"I left you," he said. "Angrily. I had myself teleported through your Barrier and into North America, where I intended to live under an assumed name and work for the overthrow of Winslow — as a start."

"Is that it?" van Alen asked. "I was never sure of your plan."

Kesley nodded. "I intended gradually to seize the Twelve Empires — and then ask you to lower your force-screen."

Van Alen smiled slowly. "Worthy of a Duke, son. But it didn't work. One of Winslow's mutant telepaths — now dead and out of circulation, happily — discovered your true identity. Word traveled fast among the Twelve Dukes that I had had a son who bore the Immortal traits. They resolved to kill you, hoping I would never have another. And you were caught, there in Winslow's own home yard. It was Daveen who rescued you. The rest you've already relearned."

Kesley nodded, calmly now. "I'm back home now, Father."

"At last. Daveen hid you so well I thought we'd

never find you. Finally I decided to go myself. I found you — and lost you again."

"You're missing my point," Kesley said sharply. "I'm back home."

"And?"

"And I haven't changed my ideas."

Van Alen slipped the electrostimulator into his hand once again and let the minute voltage caress his nerves. "So?" he said quizzically.

"I still feel the force screen ought to come down."

Van Alen shook his head frowningly. "You're not the green boy you were when you left, you know. You've seen the courts of the Dukes; you've worked on a farm. You know what it is to flee for your life."

"And I've seen Mutie City and the Colony and Wiener," Kesley added. "I've really been around."

"And?"

"And I think the world's rotten at the core! I think you can save it — if you'll only lift your damned Barrier and give what you have here to the rest of the world!"

Pain filtered over van Alen's face. He stared sadly at Kesley for a moment, with the timeless expression in his eyes that Kesley knew he, himself, would one day acquire. "You still don't understand," van Alen said huskily, "why that Barrier is up."

"No, I don't."

"You've dealt with three Immortals: Winslow, Miguel, me. What do we have in common?" van Alen demanded suddenly.

Startled, Kesley stopped to to think of their common characteristics. *Nothing in common*, he nearly answered. Then he saw he was wrong.

Physical vitality. Long life. These things were obvious.

The deepness of the eyes. Constant for all three.

And a deepness of personality, a strange complexity of behaviour, a pattern of actions appeared to be based on random selection. Yes, that was it. "You're unpredictable," Kesley said. "One never knows what to expect from you. It's as if you act without motivation sometimes."

"It seems that way, doesn't it? But look: you're lying in a tub of water, completely submerged. A hand suddenly breaks the surface of the water and plunges a knife into you. All you see is the hand; for all the evidence you have, that's all there is — just a hand."

"It's completely unmotivated, isn't it? Why would a mere hand want to murder you? No reason at all. But suppose that hand is attached to the arm of your most deadly enemy? It's not so unmotivated then, is it?"

"You mean we only see segments of events; you see the entire happening. That's it?"

"It comes with long life. You'll have it too," van Alen said. "It's a curse. You'll be living in three dimensions and everyone else in two. And no one will ever manage to understand you fully except another one like you."

"You're stalling. The Barrier," Kesley prodded.

"The Barrier. I put that up out of fear." Van Alen's strong head drooped; his ancient eyes looked bleak. "I'm safe, secure down here. We've continued to progress. No bombs were dropped on Antarctica. I don't want any bombs coming down."

"But there won't be! There can't be! They've virtually reverted to a pre-mechanical culture in the Twelve Empires. They've got as much chance of being able to build bombs as you do of sprouting wings."

A new thought occurred to Kesley. "When did you come to Antarctica? You said you'd only been ruling three hundred sixty-odd years. The Blast was more than four hundred years ago."

Van Alen seemed to be trembling. "I came to Antarctica in 2164, established control, and erected the barrier the following year." His voice wavered. "Do you want the rest of it?"

"I don't need it." Kesley jabbed a forefinger at the Duke. "You never told me this, but now I understand. 2162 — that's the year the Twelve Dukes met and divided up the world, all except Antarctica. Right?"

"Yes," van Alen said tonelessly.

"Okay. In 2162, there were twelve Empires — and *thirteen Immortals!* You were the odd man out!"

Van Alen winced, and Kesley felt a surge of pity now that he finally had voiced the words. Van Alen had lived alone with these memories for hundreds of years.

"They cast you out," Kesley went on. "You were an Immortal — it was obvious, you were a hundred years old and still in the prime of life — and everyone else grabbed a Dukedom before you did. So you slunk off to Antarctica with your tail wrapped around your hind legs, and founded yourself an Empire down here."

"No more, please," van Alen said. "Please."

"I want to go on." Kesley's eyes flashed. "You built that barrier out of fear and hatred; you closed yourself away from the Twelve who rejected you! And now —"

"And now I'm very tired," said van Alen. He rose. "Five years ago you argued for overthrowing the Barrier. I refused without citing reason. Now you understand why."

"It was because you didn't dare face your twelve old enemies," Kesley said mercilessly. "Even though Antarctica had continued scientific development and they had shunned it, even though you now had the weapons and the techniques to blast the twelve of them off their thrones at long distance, you still kept thinking of yourself as the poor relation who got shunted away. That's why you ran away when the bandits caught me in Argentina; you dreaded going before Miguel. You had to escape even at the cost of leaving me behind."

"That's part of it." Van Alen seemed to recover some of his former poise. "If you'll remember, though, I couched my refusal of your ideas five years ago in such a way that you'd almost certainly react by running away."

"I remember. Why?"

"You've seen the world. You've seen other Dukes. You know what the world is like. You've matured. It was a sink-or-swim process, and you swam."

Kesley began to see what was coming. His fingers started to tremble.

"Five years ago," van Alen went on, "I said no. Today's answer is different. It's *yes*."

Van Alen laid his still powerful hand on Kesley's shoulder. "I can't take down the Barrier myself. I need it up there, as protection — protection against emotional fears that even I know, intellectually, are foolish."

"But *you* can take it down, Dryle — as Duke of Antarctica!"

Kesley had seen it corning. He nodded. "I'm so used to thinking of myself as Dale Kesley that it's hard to remember my name's the same as yours — Dryle van Alen."

"*Dux et Imperator,*" the older man added, grinning. "A little while ago I dictated an abdication. At knife-point, to be sure, but I kept my voice calm. That message is still on the tapes. Any time you want, you have my permission to broadcast it."

Young van Alen stared evenly at his father. "The Barrier *will* come down. The Dukes will fall. I'll get Narella back from Miguel."

"These things will happen. Remember, though, there will be others after Narella. It's one of the prices you pay for long life."

"I know," he said gravely. He grinned. "I'm still young, yet, and so is she. There's time for me to start learning how to take the long view later."

He turned away and extended a hand toward the

control that would broadcast his father's message to all the continent of Antarctica.

His hand hovered for a moment.

Once, he knew, Antarctica had been covered with ice, a frozen, desolate land. Men had cleared the ice and built a garden continent.

Now, the new Duke thought, it was the other nine-tenths of the world that lay under an icy pall. That could be altered, too. The Twelve Dukes could be swept away; the walls around the cities and around men's minds could be destroyed. And it was not necessary that the tragedy of 2062 be repeated.

His finger brushed the stud and his father's words began to echo through the city and out over the entire continent.

*"People of Antarctica, hear and believe this message. Today, in the 362nd year of my rule, I am giving up my throne."*

As the abdication decree resounded through the halls of the Ducal palace, he turned and saw the robots rolling toward him, ready to give allegiance to their new lord.

He drew a deep breath. Plenty of work lay ahead. The years of the freeze were at their end; the great thaw was just beginning.

### THE END

# SPECIAL PREVIEW:

# VIXEN

## BY BUD SPARHAWK

### ARRIVAL

*Covenant*, the great, silent fish of a ship, swam silvery and smooth, slick as light, through the cold, empty dark. The dormant ship slept, but it would briefly wake to peer about to ensure that it had not deviated from its preordained path or to avoid some bit of cosmic flotsam — perhaps a vagrant comet sweeping across the arc of stars — before returning to a restless slumber. But mostly it slept through the light years as it followed the unique signature of one specific, distant star.

\*

*Cold.*

That was the first thing the Hadir, Tam Polat, became aware of: the intense cold that permeated every cell of his body, a cold that so deep that he felt as though the core of his heart was a frozen pellet, barely able to pump the slush-filled blood through his frigid veins. He strained to open his eyes, worked hard to force his eyelids to break free of their coating of ice. The shivering started long before he succeeded.

Where was he? He could barely recall something about a trip and something he had to do at the end of it, he was so cold. Oh yes, he had to remember to pick up some drinks for the people who were coming over tonight to help celebrate Solstice Day. That must be why he was so cold — winter had started and the temperature was dropping. But why did he have to pick up the drinks? He worried at the lost memory until he recalled that Larisha was bringing some new team members to see him. But what was he supposed to get? For the life of him, he couldn't remember.

God, it was cold!

Tam's shivering became more intense. Must have fallen through the ice, he thought. Wasn't there a pond or stream he had to cross to get home? A fall into winter waters would be a shock to his body. Perhaps he was in the hospital and they were trying to bring him back to life. Would Doctor Chen be there, hovering over him, coaxing him back from the brink?

No, Chen wouldn't be in the emergency ward of the local hospital. He was on the departure team. Why had he thought that Doctor Chen should be here, wherever here was?

The ice that held his eyelids tight finally gave way, and he blinked at the bright lights shining down on him, on his steaming, naked body. Why had they left him lying here without clothing or even a decent blanket to warm him? Didn't anybody in this hospital care about . . .

But the ceiling wasn't that of any hospital he'd ever seen. Too close, too blue, too slick and shining, it looked like nothing more than the inside lid of a food container.

Something clicked, as if a floe had broken loose, releasing his memories. Sudden clarity flooded his mind with certain knowledge of this place, this time, and the critical rôle he was destined to play upon revival.

This was no hospital. There had been no accident, no fall into icy waters. The Solstice Day he'd remembered was years, perhaps centuries in the past. No, this chill awakening had nothing to do with an accident, but Doctor Chen had most definitely been involved. Doctor Chen had put Tam into this chamber. Doctor Chen had frozen him for the long one-way trip.

A few moments more and his eyes finally adjusted to the lights . . . the radiant lamps warming his body, bringing him back up to normal temperature. He could feel the warmth seeping into his bones, thawing the core of ice at his center, melting the years of stasis away, drop by drop; a snowflake of months here, a snowbank of frozen years there, and a century's icicle, all flowing away as life returned and the flurry of pelting minutes began.

The shivering finally ceased, his fingers and toes stopped tingling, and he became aware of a great thirst. His throat was parched. Something insistently prodded his right cheek. He turned his head and noticed a thin tube at mouth level moving back and forth. As he opened his lips, the tube slid smoothly forward, and a trickle of warm broth ran over his tongue and down his throat. He gagged for a second and then remembered to swallow. The hot fluid coursed through him, warming his insides and restoring his strength.

"Take it slowly," he recalled Doctor Chen cautioning during the indoctrination sessions. "You must work your way back to life with great care. One does not abuse the body after so long a sleep." Good advice. If the trip had gone according to profile, he would have been in stasis for, at a minimum, nearly two hundred years.

Two hundred years! My God, Doctor Chen would probably be dead by now, as would most of those who had prepared the crew for the voyage. He wished he could thank them for the excellent job they'd done to ensure his survival, but that would be impossible, given the exigencies of interstellar travel. No, they would have already gotten whatever rewards they'd deserved, died, and been forgotten, along with everything else he had known. All that was calendar and light years in the past. None of them were any longer his concern.

When the radiant lamps clicked off, Tam slid the cover away with stiff and aching arms before drifting across the cold chamber to the lockers. He struggled to straighten himself, his muscles protesting their long disuse. Finally, with an effort of will, he reached a locker, opened it, and pulled out a thick coverall. After struggling for agonizing moments with stiffened fingers, he got himself dressed. With still greater effort, he put warm stockings on his feet to protect them from the chill of the deck.

His glandular balancing was still going on. He simultaneously felt joy and sorrow, lassitude and exhilaration, always out of step with his raging emotions. Manic energy fought against a crushing depression for a few seconds while, a heartbeat later, beaming optimism battled lassitude.

"Wait the emotional storm out," Chen had cautioned. "It will pass."

He made a half turn and lowered himself into his seat, pressed two buttons, and waited as the unit heated three steaming mugs to restore the nutrients that his body had lost. Chen's insistent protocol demanded that he down them all before starting work.

"It will do the others no good if you, uh, expire before you can attend to their needs."

Doctor Chen had sounded as though he were lecturing on manners instead of a life-saving, life-restoring procedure. But he would follow the old doctor's advice. He would do as he was taught. One did not lightly ignore the advice of the wise. One did not ignore the orders of the Hand of God's chief scientist.

The liquid in the first mug tasted salty. Tam suspected that it was designed to restore his electrolyte balance. The second was so sweet that he could barely get it down — sugar for quick energy, he thought, as his brain began to function normally.

The contents of the third mug were a surprise — warm, dark chocolate, just the way he liked it. He savored the taste. It might be the last chocolate he'd have for years. Good old Chen, ever the considerate one.

Memory returned with a rush. He was the Hadir, Tam Polat, in command of the Hand of God's own ship — *Covenant* — on its voyage from Heaven to Meridian. He was to prepare the way for the wave of settlers who would arrive fifty years behind him. His mission was to survive, to exploit whatever resources he found, and to have this system ready for colonization. He had the authority and means to do anything and everything necessary to that end.

Within an hour, Tam felt much stronger and, with the strengthening nourishment inside him, he began the arduous process of bringing the Raggi, Bul Larisha, his second in command, out of stasis. He unpacked blankets to wrap her in when she awoke.

"Best that the people not face the indignity of waking naked," Doctor Chen had said. The psychological support provided by the thick warm blankets was as important as the physical benefit, he'd insisted.

But Tam didn't care about that. All he really cared about at the moment was that the blankets would help Larisha revive faster so she could de-ice enough of the crew to warm this ship and rid it of the stink of too many years, too many chemicals, and too few human activities.

After he had started the restoration process for Larisha, he wormed his way to the command module through the tightly-packed bags, boxes, and containers of supplies that filled every compartment and corridor. The module was cold as the grave, still recovering from the near-absolute-zero of the emptiness between the stars. He touched the toggle that would open the observation port's cover, but did not flip it on.

This was an historic moment, one that no one in this system would experience for another thousand years, when the next wave of the expansion left. He wanted to savor it, to burn it into his mind forever.

But there was something else staying his hand. He felt as if he were under observation. He felt as if God Himself were watching his actions — as if he were being weighed by something far beyond his ken.

"Emerging God, I am Your faithful servant," he intoned. "I will justify Your trust in me. I will do the work of the Hand as You directed." The simple declaration of faith gave him comfort. He would have been remiss had he allowed his hubris to make him forget his rôle, his humble place in God's plan. He flipped the cold toggle, hardly breathing, as the cover began to withdraw.

His first impression was of a huge expanse of blinding white. Then he noticed the other colors, the full spectrum of subtle shades. The complexity of form, the infinite depths.

He screamed in fright. His worse fears had been realized.

God was watching him.

When Tam Polat recovered from shock, only bright stars sparked on the deep velvet field of the heavens. None of the configurations was familiar. A single star, brighter than all the rest, blazed off to one side. It had to be their target. They had arrived.

He shivered. Had the apparition been a transient effect of the drugs, or had he actually been blessed to see the true face of God? He recalled the apparition with such intensity, such clarity, that he knew it could not have been a figment of his imagination. No, his perceptions, his memories of that sight, were too vivid. It must have happened. He was blessed indeed.

He was still trembling from that awesome feeling of being examined, weighed, and then discarded as if unworthy of notice. He prayed that the other Men would be spared such a degrading experience.

But why had he been so blessed? Perhaps he, as leader of their enterprise, as the Hadir of Heaven's mission, had been granted the boon of seeing a tiny piece of God's greater glory. Perhaps it had been a reward, an affirmation of his historic rôle.

Yes, that was the only explanation. Heaven's Hand had chosen well. He *was* truly blessed.

With renewed strength, he turned to continue his work.

# ONE

A full week after emerging from the long freeze, Tam was still amazed at how easily he tired after such a long and peaceful sleep. Of course, it was very easy to tire in the chill air of the ship — air that still stank of machine sterility and dust too-long undisturbed. He shivered once more and rubbed his arms to help his circulation. Surely time would cure him of this weakness.

According to the schedule, Larisha's Halfings, the maintenance crew in particular, were supposed to have the environmental units operating by now. That should have produced a little heat and provided some relief. So why couldn't he detect any warm air coming through the vents in the command module? How long must he wait before he felt a change in the temperature?

But that was a foolish question. For two hundred years or more the ship had been a hairsbreadth above the ambient temperature of interstellar space. Even with the ship's heaters going full blast, it would take a long, long time before these cold walls and decks grew warm. With a sigh over matters even he, as the mission's supreme ruler — Hadir — could not control, he pulled his heavy parka around him and turned his attention to other matters.

Thus far, things had gone according to plan, with no more crises than expected: A few systems had failed over their long years of disuse; some of the crew members hadn't survived stasis; and the hull had suffered minor damage from debris encountered during the long voyage. But all of these events had been anticipated, and contingency plans had been made. Repairs, replacements, and disposal were quickly accomplished.

Larisha had already de-iced more of the Halfing technicals and had them preparing the living quarters for the others who would soon be revived. Preparing the spartan quarters took time; time to find the necessary connections, determine the proper fittings, and locate the appropriate tools.

The Halfings's stumbling confusion and their initially slow progress had been expected. The lower orders didn't have the same constitution as the Men. It would be a while before they recovered from their long sleep. Give them time to adjust and grow strong and things would become normal, Larisha insisted.

Once Larisha's Halfings had the ship more liveable, he could bring his trusted Outriders and their Scouts out of deep freeze. He always intended to have enough of Men to control Larisha's Halfings and their mongrels. It wouldn't do to let the ship's population get too much out of balance.

Tam had been working hard since his shivering arousal from the long, sleepless night. He'd spent most of his time since awakening in revising the de-icing schedules and going over the ship's data about this star system with Outrider Gull Tamat, his science advisor. He had to learn as much as possible before he acted. He wasn't going to select which of the several mission options he was going to implement until he knew more about this system.

Tamat, the head of the science team, had already charted three gas giants in the system. One of them — which Gull had named Thetti, after the Prophet's mother — was visible from the ship. It was the sixth from the primary, which had been named Hannah.

Heaven's astronomers had been quite correct in their long range appraisal of this system: Meridian, the name chosen for their destination, was the only habitable planet. At present that destination was on the other side of Hannah. Meridian had been briefly visible to the ship's sensors as they approached from galactic west, perpendicular to this system's ecliptic. They were now, according to the ship's records, running parallel to the orbit of Meridian and already slowing to match its pace and begin their descent to its orbit.

Tam watched the bright, ruddy globe of Thetti and its constellation of seven satellites swim across the command module's observation port. Thetti would be rich in resources they could exploit to supplement their diminishing stores.

But mining the gas giant was only one of several supporting options to prepare the way for settlers. He could, as one option, build a space habitat — the beginnings of a base from which the settlers could exploit this system's resources. A habitat would have been his choice had Heaven's astronomers proven incorrect. But, since Meridian appeared to be a habitable planet, he could exercise his second option: bypass the gas giants and make a direct approach. It was his choice alone, although, for form's sake, he would seek the support of the Men's Council — his trusted lieutenants — and, he added ruefully — that of Dalgrun Wofat, Palm of the Hand of God, ship's religious leader, and a huge pain in the ass.

But the support of those Men would only be a formality. As

the ship's Hadir, as its absolute leader, he could and would select whichever option he felt would best serve God's plan, with or without their permission. Such was the authority given directly to him by the Hand of Heaven, practically directly from God. No one could dispute his decisions. His encounter with God himself only reënforced his certainty. He could not choose wrong.

He continued watching the bright dot of Thetti and the lights closest to it. Some of those lights were moons and some were stars, but which were which? He could not tell without a telescope or Gull's expert assistance. One of the points of light sparkled with a spectrum of color and reminded him of his vision. God as a crystal being — what a strange form for him to have taken.

As he stared, the sparkling star began to move. He jerked to full alert, wondering what it might be; there were no shuttles or scoops deployed as yet. Had one of the Halfings working outside the hull drifted loose? Could it be some hapless worker's suit lights? There were few referents to gauge distances in the starry sky.

The dot swiftly brightened and faded. In less than a second, it was completely gone.

Tam let out his breath, his heart racing, his mind awhirl. How could the light simply disappear? Where could it have gone? What had it been? He tried to recall some details of what he had seen in that fraction of a second, but could not make sense of that all-to-brief glimpse.

"What the hell happened?" he demanded as he slapped the communications console's TRANSMIT button. "That crystal light — did anyone else see where it went? Report!"

At that moment, Gull Tamat pulled himself into Tam's cramped command center. Gull was a swarthy Man, the same height as Tam, although with longer legs. Gull's dark hair was nearly black, and he tied it back in a knot typical of the fashion of Man's cadre. He differed from Tam and the rest of the Men in only a few details: His bright brown eyes always held a hint of hidden amusement, with a smile lurking about their corners. It was as if he alone held the punch line of some amusing joke.

"What's happening, Hadir?" he said. "What's the matter?"

"There was a light that just disappeared," Tam said. He stared down at the indicators from the ship's sensors. "It was there one minute ago. Right near the edge of the planet, damn it!"

"Hmmm, I don't see anything out of the ordinary." Gull leaned over Tam and peered out. "Did you say this thing passed out of sight behind Thetti?"

"Damn it, it didn't pass out of sight. It disappeared! Check and see if you can find something that would confirm what I saw. The sensors must have captured a record of its disappearance. There was no way an event like that could have evaded detection."

The responses to Tam's panicked cross-ship transmission started to come in. Station after station reported nothing out of the ordinary.

"That may not be indicative," Gull Tamat said dryly. "All of the people working on the hull were on the side facing away from Thetti."

"Then they wouldn't have seen it," Tam said at once.

Gull listened to the reports, nodding. "I agree. It looks as if you were the only observer, Hadir Polat." Then curiosity got the better of him. "But you said 'crystal.' Why did you mean by that?"

Tam hesitated, trying to sort out the confusing image, "Did I say that? How strange." He let the comment hang. On reflection, he doubted if he could really say it was a crystal with any degree of certainty. "I believe I was thinking that the light was sparkling — crystal-like. Perhaps that is why I said it."

"Perhaps something reflected off the hull in the glass." Gull continued to peer through the observation port.

Tam nodded slowly. "Yes, perhaps." Still, the instruments and the outside observers hadn't reported anything. "I guess we can't deny the evidence, can we?"

The scientist checked the instruments once more, just to make sure. "Yes, it must have been a reflection. I wouldn't worry about it."

Then Gull looked closely at Tam. "On the other hand, your strong reaction to something so trivial could be a sign that you are overly tired. Perhaps that is why you were so easily mistaken. I suggest that you get some sleep. You've been pushing yourself far too much."

When Tam didn't change his expression, Gull continued.

"Hadir Polat, listen to me. Everything appears to be well in hand at the moment. Larisha and the others have the Halfings working hard. We're starting to de-ice some Folk, and their help will help us restore the ship to full operation. Please take it easier on yourself. Some rest would give you a clear head."

Tam slowly nodded. "You may be right, Gull. I haven't been sleeping that well lately." He forced a laugh. "It's probably because of the damn cold. All right, I will do just as you advise, old friend. We can discuss what you have learned of this system later, after I get some of your suggested rest." With those words, he waved Gull away.

But the memory of the light nagged him as he transferred temporary command to the Raggi. Had it only been a reflection, or had it been real? Should he believe his own senses, should he honor his own memory, or should he accept the solid evidence of the sensors, not to mention the reports from the crew?

The question vexed him until he fell into an uneasy sleep.

*

Gull Tamat looked completely confident as he stood before

Tam and the Men's council.

"I have perused the ship's records in great depth and conclude that this is a very rich system," he announced. "Our people should be able to exploit its resources for centuries to come.

"First, Meridian is exactly what our astronomers predicted. It has an atmosphere that is nearly Earth-normal, so we'll only have to make a few adjustments, perhaps do some atmospheric seeding to adjust the mix of gases, so that, by the time the settlers arrive, we'll have a decent planet waiting for them."

"You said this is a rich system. What are its resources?" Tam interrupted.

Gull pursed his lips. "The three gas giants are useful. Thetti, the nearest one, has the greatest potential. Its atmosphere is rich in gases we can use to fabricate the materials we'll need. It also has a large amount of particulate matter suspended in its clouds. If I were to choose which of the three gas giants we should mine, I would strongly recommend Thetti."

Tam considered that assessment. "I would have thought the distribution of resources would be a little more equitable."

Gull hesitated. "The others are good candidates, but they are pretty far out from the primary and are rather cold. I would say that we'd have to work much harder to extract anything of value from them. No, Hadir Polat, Thetti is our best bet." He hesitated for a moment and then added. "That is, if you decide to use it to build up our store of resources before heading to Meridian."

"I have not yet decided," Tam said curtly. "For the moment, I am considering all options equally. Now, tell us more about Thetti. I want to know about those seven moons. Are they of any use to us?"

"Um . . ." Gull shifted uncomfortably. He was clearly nervous and ill-at-ease over this question.

"Well," Tam said, "surely you've collected *some* information on the Prophet's mother's sisters, haven't you?"

A few of the Men laughed at Tam's joke.

"Six moons, Hadir Polat," Gull Tamat said slowly. "There are only six moons around Thetti."

Tam frowned. "You initially reported seven moons. Were you mistaken?"

Gull coughed, a nervous little explosion that was clearly forced. "I suspect that there was some error in the astronomical instruments. A bit of noise introduced during our long passage, perhaps. We are searching for the reason."

Tam sensed something amiss. He had known Gull too long. The Man was never uncertain. And he seldom, if ever, made a mistake of this magnitude. Best to pursue this matter later, in private. No point in embarrassing the scientist before this crowd.

"Fine, so we now have doubtful data," Tam said irritably. "Please recheck all other readings, so we can be sure of what is really out there." He settled back. "Now, why don't you tell us what information you *think* you know."

Gull continued, clearly stung by the mild rebuke.


Three days later, Gull approached Tam with a sheaf of reports in his hands. "Do you have a moment?" he asked, a strange note in his voice.

"What's the matter?" Tam growled without slowing his progress. "Tell me on the way to the engine compartment. There's some sort of difficulty with the mains I have to look into."

"Nothing serious, I hope," Gull replied as he tagged along.

"Bringing the ship up to livable conditions isn't proceeding according to plan. Larisha told me there's some glitch in expanding the ring around the center of the ship." Tam threaded his way through a hatch. "The ship's slow rotation is making some of the crew sick."

"I know what you mean," Gull said. "This gravitational differential between head and feet would make anyone ill." He rubbed his belly to indicate the area of distress.

Tam paused. "Really? It doesn't bother me all that much. But that doesn't matter. The inadequate rotation is slowing the pace of getting the ship completed and therefore has to be fixed."

Through the morning he'd worked with Larisha to decide on which experts they had to de-ice to supplement the Halfings technicians she already had on hand. Somehow the Man who had been trained for this complicated task hadn't been placed high enough on the revival list — another stupid manifest mistake some witless clerk back on Heaven had made. He wished that he could have that clerk here now, freezing his ass off and throwing up on a regular basis. Regardless, those without his iron belly would have to suffer another day or two until the expert was up and about.

"What was it you wanted to talk about?" he asked the scientist as they squeezed between the sacks of supplies that had been stuffed into every available space on the ship. Once they had the ship expanded there would be more room — if the ship ever was expanded, he added pessimistically.

The ship's belly was a ring of compressed foil which, when forced out by the ship's rapid rotation, would expand into a ring nearly half a kilometer in diameter. At the same time the forward and aft sections would be moved slowly apart. This move would form the expanding ring into a fat disk. It was tedious and precise work fraught with risk, which was why they needed the Man who had been trained for this.

Once the ring was formed the workers would divide the disk's interior into corridors, compartments, work rooms, laboratories, and mechanical rooms. The ship would become, if everything went right, a small city.

"I just wanted you to know that we've finished checking

the astronomical instruments that were malfunctioning." Gull squeezed past bulging sacks of vacuum-dried fruits.

Tam arrested his forward motion by placing one hand against a container of figs. He turned to face the scientist.

"*Were* malfunctioning? Just what do you mean by that? Has it put the ship in danger? My God, why didn't you tell me about this earlier?"

Gull held up his hands in protest. "No, the malfunction wasn't that serious, I assure you. Nothing that directly affected the ship's performance. No, Hadir Polat, this was more subtle than that."

"Well, what is it, then?" Tam demanded. "Come on, you don't bring something to my attention and then dismiss it as trivial. I know you better than that. Hell, I chose you myself for that very trait! Now, tell me."

"It was the long-range astronomical instruments," Gull explained quietly. "Apparently, the systemic noise in them was enough to indicate that there were five major satellites orbiting Thetti and two smaller moons. We've checked and rechecked the original readings and can only locate six of them now. One of the smaller ones seems to have, uh, disappeared."

Tam pursed his lips in thought. "That is very strange. I can't believe that you've lost an entire moon."

The scientist looked embarrassed. "I didn't say that we lost it. As I said before, it must have been some noise in the system, some bright blips that we interpreted as a minor satellite. It isn't as if we actually lost it," he concluded plaintively.

Tam laughed at the Man's fallen face. "Don't be so upset, Gull. I was just joking. It's not your fault that one of the moons disappeared." He smiled to show that this too was a joke, but Gull Tamat interpreted it differently.

"It wasn't a moon," he repeated angrily. "I told you that it was an anomaly — some bad data, was all."

"So why are you concerned enough to come to me?" Tam asked. "If it was an error that no longer exists why should it concern me?"

Gull rattled his papers again. "It seems that the last mistaken record was made just a few days ago.

"So?" Tam smiled politely. He was growing weary of the scientist's inability to come to the point.

"It seems that the malfunctioning instrument stopped malfunctioning around the same time you reported seeing that disappearing star."

Tam stopped immediately. "Are you saying that the two events are related? What I saw was a reflection of something near the ship. It must have been something small and close, not a damn moon, for God's sake!"

Gull grinned. "You have a good grasp of reality, Hadir Polat. All right, so the two events aren't related. It would be impossible for the moon to have been what you say you saw. Quite impossible."

"A coincidence, that's all it was, Outrider. A silly, chance coincidence."

Gull nodded in agreement. "Yes, you must certainly be right, Hadir Polat. I stand corrected. I am sorry to have troubled you."

Tam slapped the scientist on the shoulder. "No trouble, old friend. But keep your crew looking for that malfunction just the same. I want absolute assurance that our instruments are doing what they're supposed to. Absolute assurance!"

"As you wish Hadir Tam Polat," Gull bowed obedience. "As you instruct."

Tam tried to think no more of the matter for the rest of the day. But Gull's lost moon came to mind later, as he was resting in the quiet of his bunk. He thought about the bright crystal essence of God that he'd seen through the port. He thought about the tiny disappearing star, the one that all of the instruments and all of the possible observers had said hadn't happened. Had it really been something near Thetti? Could that have been the missing "moon" despite the obvious impossibility of it all?

He played with that thought. Was such a thing just too fantastic to believe? Wouldn't Gull Tamat's instruments detect something moon-sized if it disappeared? He'd supposed it to be a small object, as Gull had insisted at the time, but it could have been farther away — it could have been a moon-sized item circling Thetti!

Then he shook himself. A moon, even a small one, could not break the laws of physics. God did not play kick-ball with astronomy, at least not in real time! No, if the moon had existed at all, then it would surely have registered on the instruments. The disappearance of anything that size would probably have perturbed the ship's path a measurable degree as well.

He'd only had that briefest of glimpses and still wasn't sure of the memory. Gull must have been correct; it had been nothing more than a chance reflection, a trick of the eye, a phantasm. And a coincidence as well.

Besides, a moon would not resemble a crystal.


The repairs to the main engines required nothing more than replacement of a minor part that had frozen sometime during the cold years and someone who could authorize the work. He cursed. For that they'd had to lose three days of progress. Briefly, Tam wished that they had enough leisure time that he could apply some much needed discipline to the workers. Nothing motivated the Halfings like a good public whipping. By God, if he were back on Heaven with a squad of good horse behind him, they'd not dare . . .

But they were not on Heaven. His beloved grassy plains were far behind them, and enough horses for a squad could not be bred in this system for years. Until then, his Men had to walk about like common people, like the damned mongrels.

Thanks to the repair job, the ship's revolution gradually stabilized so that the ring could be extended from where it had laid collapsed, like a thick belt, around the mid-line of the ship. The crew immediately began filling the newly created space with supplies and machinery from the storage spaces in the main ship. This shifted considerable mass from the ship's center and gradually slowed the speed of the ship's revolution.

Finally, a decent degree of artificial gravity was achieved at the rim. Work on the ship proceeded without further incident.

The ship's engines remained still as the crew waited for their Hadir to tell them which option he would choose. Everyone knew that there was sufficient fuel remaining in the tanks to reach and orbit Meridian. The need to reach their destination, to walk on the surface of a planet once again, to start to build for the future, was palpable throughout the ship.

Yet, they also knew that prudence argued mightily for orbiting Thetti and mining its depths. That would ensure them of enough reserves to handle any contingency. Hadn't the Hadir publicly stated that replenishing their fuel before proceeding would be the wisest choice?

There was also a third option: to build a habitat, an orbiting refuge, just in case something untoward should occur as they tried to conquer Meridian. Perhaps, some mused as they awaited the Hadir's decision, he would choose a combination of the three.

Tam was still uneasy in dealing with Bul Larisha: his Raggi, leader of the Halfings, his former lover, his official wife. The presence of Larisha on the ship was something that he regretted. At one time, she had seemed such a perfect candidate. Not only was she a loyal follower of the Hand of God, but was an excellent Man in other respects. Brilliant and witty, with excellent technical, academic, and political credentials, Larisha had passed every test and met every criteria the Hand had set for those in command positions. Of her capability for the rôle, there was no doubt. She had also declared to Heaven's Hand her warmest desire to spread the seed of Man throughout the universe. He himself, the Hadir of the Meridian *Covenant*, had endorsed her inclusion vigorously, declaring her the best stock that Men had to offer.

Which was perfectly understandable. At that time, he had been deeply in love with her. At that time, he had not yet asked her to marry him. At that time, he had thought that they were going to ride together in God's great plan to extend Man's dominion over the universe. At that time, he'd not known her failings.

Or his own. . . .

---

*Read the rest of*

# VIXEN

## BY BUD SPARHAWK

*Available now*
*wherever Cosmos Books are sold.*

ISBN: 978-0-8439-5945-1 / U.S. $6.99.